"I'm a professional," said Harb. "It took me less than fourteen months on that world before I was promoted to Sector Chief and transferred to this sector to replace your old chief. Fourteen months — not ten years."

"What of it?"

"What of it?" repeated Harb. "It means that I was successful on my world. I got results. I stuck my neck out to get them, but I got them. And I got patted on the back for them, not court-martialed. . . . The higher echelons at Earth Headquarters don't live by your rule book. They can't afford to. Behind that rule book the law is survival of the fittest. If you have the brains and the guts to break the rules, but get what's wanted in the process, the fact that you broke the rules is going to be overlooked. I intend to get what's wanted."

This is the first FULLY ILLUSTRATED Ace novel, ready to take you inside the world of a real **PRO**

This book is for Ben Bova,
a friend for all seasons.

SF

GORDON R. DICKSON
PRO

Illustrated by James R. Odbert

ace books
A Division of Charter Communications Inc.
A GROSSET & DUNLAP COMPANY
360 Park Avenue South
New York, New York 10010

PRO

An ACE Book

First Ace printing: October 1978

Printed in U.S.A.

"...There was no suspicion
in the mind of any
that the Duke himself
was responsible for the death
of Facino. It was simply
that Facino's death created
a situation only to be met by
the destruction of the Duke..."

BELLARION, by Rafael Sabatini

PROLOGUE

To Bill Cohone, who was unimportant, news came late and the supervisory people in his Sector came by infrequently. One exception to this, however, was Major Manai Elles, the Medical Services officer. Manai dropped in whenever she could.

Cohone left his quarters and walked out to meet the shuttle that had just brought her down from the permanent orbital station at which her ship would have parked and which was his single link with the rest of humanity. The port had opened in the side of the shuttle and she was on her way out before he reached her. Her arms were full of mail, including one fairly good-sized package — an unusual sight, considering the distance World 49381D was from Earth, and the cost of sending anything larger than a letter this far.

"Presents," she called to him as she turned to greet him. In her white slacks and shirt, with only the Med Service badge for color on the pocket, she was a vibrant sight. Her hair was as black as obsidian, black enough to catch the rich yellow light of the sun in glints of warm fire. She was tall, slim and — Cohone reminded himself again — fourteen years younger than he was. He had never understood why she seemed to like him.

"What's in the package?" he asked, unloading her.

"You're supposed to tell me." Her ceaselessly brilliant eyes held him merrily. "It's from your publisher, isn't it?"

Cohone's gaze suddenly recognized the sign of the publishing firm he had dealt with.

"Oh. That."

"What is it?"

Abruptly, her voice was concerned. She hooked an arm in one of his now laden ones and turned him toward his quarters.

"They've sent me a couple of copies of my book," he told her as they went. "I've been expecting it."

In the main room of the quarters, Cohone opened the package, to display two disposable film-players with the title OTHER WAYS THAN OURS in star-glitter on the dark blue of each front panel. His name was also there, in glitter but in very small print.

"It means they've decided to trash the unsold copies. Yes," he went on, reading the note that had accompanied the two copies, "that's what they say here. I was expecting this."

"Trash!" the major was outraged. "It's only been out five months."

"Well, it's a financial decision on their parts, of course. It just didn't find enough buyers . . ."

"Because they didn't try hard enough. That's their job!"

"Oh, I suppose they tried." Cohone laid the two books aside, gently in spite of his tone of indifference. "They have to make decisions like that on a lot of the books they publish."

4

"It's a book they shouldn't ever trash — a book a lot of people back there ought to be reading. There isn't one in a million back there who appreciate the realities we deal with out here."

He looked toward her, loving her — though of course he would never be idiot enough to tell her so. Luckily, behind her head, he suddenly caught sight of his own reflection in the turned-off communications screen built into the far wall, and the ghostly image of his own tall, balding, round-faced self sobered him with its reminder of other realities.

"Well, if I ever make a name for myself, I can try to get it republished," he said.

"You will," she told him.

He laughed.

"Forget the book," he said. "Tell me the news."

"The news — " Manai's voice changed. "We've got a new Sector Chief, and he'll be visiting you any day now."

"New Sector Chief?"

"A man named Harb Mallard. He's one of the Academy wonders — what they call a full-fledged professional. Apparently he completely revamped the last Sector he handled. Don't let him push you around, now."

Cohone smiled.

"All right. I won't."

"I mean that," she said. "You do let people push you around."

"No," he sobered suddenly. "In fact, I don't — not when it gets down to something important."

She looked at him doubtfully.

Shuttling down from the permanent orbital station to the world known as 49381D, the man named Harb Mallard, who was important, found a fair-sized clearing on the narrow, pebbled shore of a wide, gray lake combed with rolling waves running from half a dozen winding, water-miles away.

A cool wind blew from the lake, for evidently it was only the beginning of a spring, here. Across the clearing was one large building, clearly a sort of warehouse, and a number of smaller ones, all of cream-color bubble plastic. Beside the buildings, stretching to the green-gray tangled forest wall, were planted fields with the bare inches-high green stubble of winter-sown grain in rows. Hoeing among the rows were four stooped and hairy figures wearing body, arm and leg wrappings of

brown or scarlet cloth, and one human with no shirt on his skinny upper body, his half-bald scalp shining redly in the pumpkin-yellow sunlight. Ideal, thought Harb, and went to meet the man.

The man, having seen the transfer-pod land and Harb emerge, was already yelling at his workers, snatching up a shirt and hat and abandoning his hoe. He came toward Harb, sweating, dressing as he came.

"You must be Mallard!" he said warmly, offering a dirty hand which Harb shook — with no distaste but with a certain sense of irony. "I'm Bill Cohone — but you know that, of course. Come on in. Come on in — you could stand a drink, I suppose ..." Chattering cheerfully, and stuffing his shirt into his pants as he went, he led Harb into the large building, ushered him to a seat, and got them both brandy and water in blackish clay cups.

"Don't you have an overseer to head up the work in the fields, instead of being out there yourself?" Harb asked him.

"They won't keep at it unless I'm with them — the Homskarters, I mean." Cohone grinned and seated himself. He was, thought Harb, exactly what his records had indicated — an obvious volunteer, with more idealism than brains.

"Not very tame, then, are they?" Harb said.

"Well — they're independents. You know how the survey tagged them." Cohone gave a helpless shrug. "I get the ones nobody wants among their own people. The old rice-Christian business." He shrugged again, and spoke apologetically in the candid confessional tone of one talking with a fellow worker. "I'm just sort of a caretaker, here, anyway. I suppose you know I'm a volunteer?"

"Yes," said Harb. He did not bother to rub it in. The breed of man before him was dying out in the Expansion Service. Men of Harb's stamp were taking over, professional xenosociologists, thought Harb, who were not content to sit and wait for the natives of promising worlds like this one to invite human help. Statistics sounded good, but too often they left you with a hole in your pocket and only a string of impressive figures for comfort.

Harb finished his drink.

"I wish I'd been able to get out here before this," he said, "but the past year since I took over as Sector Chief things have kept me close to Sector Headquarters. I notice the records say you've been here ten local years. That's longer than any volunteer or professional I've got planted on a probable world in my sector. And this is all you've got to show for it?"

The cheerful lines in Cohone's face slowly smoothed out and faded. He stared, with his jaw slack and mouth open slightly. It was the exact expression that would have accompanied a flush of anger and embarrassment in a younger man. But age and sunburn had robbed Bill Cohone of this ability.

"You ought to see the crowds I get on Mondays — that's my medical day," he answered slowly. "And the four Homskarters you see out there aren't the only ones I've had. I've had dozens. They stay a while and then go back to their people. There's a lot of good feeling for us among them. I mean — among the rank and file. Naturally, the kings and chieftains don't lean to us, yet. They don't need us like the plain people do."

"But they're the ones you've got to convince,"

said Harb, coolly. "Aren't they?"

Cohone stared at him. Slowly his mouth closed and his jaw tightened. The earlier warmth and camaraderie of his greeting was all gone.

"They're warriors," he said grimly. "Plunderers. Fighting and feasting's all they know. And you want me to tell them to get out and sweat behind a plow? You ought to know they're the last to be convinced of that. I have to start with the bottom ranks and work up. You must know the survey!"

"The survey made of this planet," said Harb, quietly, "was set up to chart a course of action for you, not for you to hide behind."

Cohone glared at him plainly, now.

"I'm not hiding behind it — you know that!" he snapped. "But I've been here ten years. You haven't. These people are independents — *independents*, you understand? And independent cultures are like rubber balls, you punch them and they punch back automatically."

"Yes, I know," interrupted Harb, dryly. "I've seen that book you wrote."

"Then you ought to realize the culture differences among these aliens here! We have to understand these Homskarters. They can't be forced. You've got to convince them. And that's a slow process, maybe taking local generations to change. No one could make that slow process move any faster than I've made it move here; and that's all there is to it. You can't *force* change on independent culture."

"There's more than one kind of force," said Harb, still quietly. He sat back, and let his words sink in. He saw the loosening of Cohone's features into an expression like despair.

"You're recommending my removal then?" Cohone said, at last. "That's what you're here for?"

"Not at all," said Harb. "I'm here to help you. Come along."

He led the way back out to the transfer boat. From the boat he brought out equipment and dressed himself. When he was done, he stood before Cohone, armed not only with a handgun, but with a Homskarter-style sword and a concave shield having a spike in the center. A backpack, rations belt, and outdoor clothing — from high boots to a crash helmet disguised as a Homskarter conical iron helm — completed his outfit.

"But you'll make trouble!" said Cohone almost fiercely when the dressing was completed. "All that stuff's too advanced to use here. It's illegal! When Earth HQ learns about this, they'll convict you —"

"They'll commend me, not convict me," said Harb, dryly. He looked at the other man with what was almost a touch of pity. "Tell me, what did you do before you volunteered?"

"I was a bridge engineer — a managing bridge engineer!" said Cohone. "I've worked with people like these locals on physical jobs all my life —"

"But," said Harb, "you wanted to do something worthwhile, and real. So you signed up and they gave you a three-month course in the basics of xenosociology and the rules in the Handbook; and for the last ten years you've been here trying to make it work the way you were taught."

"What's wrong with that?"

"Nothing," said Harb. "For a volunteer like yourself. But I'm a professional. I have two degrees and one of them is in xenosociology. On top of that, I've had four years of Academy training, and a six-month internship at Earth Headquarters before I was sent out to take a post on a probable world, like this one. It took me less than fourteen months on that world before I was promoted to Sector Chief and transferred to this sector to replace your old chief. Fourteen months — not ten years."

"What of it?"

"What of it?" repeated Harb. "It means that I was successful on my probable world. I got results. And I didn't get them by working the way you've done here. I stuck my neck out to get them, but I got them. And I got patted on the back for them, not court-martialed. Do you know why?"

"No," retorted Cohone, "and if there is a reason, it's got to be a bad one."

"Good or bad depends on your point of view," said Harb. "The higher echelons at Earth Headquarters don't live by your rule book. They can't afford to. Behind that rule book the law is survival of the fittest. If you have the brains and the guts to break the rules, but get what's wanted in the process, the fact that you broke the rules is going to be overlooked. I intend to get what's wanted."

"And what's that?" Cohone's face was lumpy and savage.

Harb shook his head at him.

"You really don't understand?" he said. "All right, I'll tell you. I've got a dozen worlds in my sector and a dozen people like you on them; but the other eleven are showing worthwhile results. I'm not going to let the record of this one planet pull down my overall achievement report. So, I'm here to help you out. All on my own. You don't have to break a rule or do a thing. I'll do it."

"But what?" demanded Cohone. "What're you going to do?"

"What's necessary. The situation's too static, and you haven't been able to move the locals out of that in ten years. We've got to shake up the status quo here, or this station of yours can sit forever with your medical days and your rice-Christian local converts, and nothing's going to happen. Now — where do you keep your boats?"

He picked up a small, power-unit-operated out-board thruster — absolutely forbidden for culture levels such as obtained here.

Grimly silent, Cohone led him down along the pebbled beach to a small floating dock to which were tied a number of the high-sided native boats — canots, they had been named in the sur-vey, after the Canadian-French word for canoe.

These were all as narrow as splinters, with tall prows and sterns. Harb picked the one which seemed to have the most beam to it, and stepped carefully down into it. Seating himself, he clipped the outboard motor to its right side near the stern, with the motor's jet down in the water; and cast off.

"I still say — you don't understand!" burst out Cohone suddenly behind him, as he drifted away from the dock. "I've put ten years of my life into this station! You can't do this to it!"

"You can't. But I can," answered Harb half to himself and switched the motor on. The burbling of its jet soon covered the sound of Cohone's now shouting voice, as man, dock and clearing dwin-dled into the shoreline distance behind the stern of the canot.

Harb set a course from point to point of the wavering shoreline, and the little canot sliced smoothly, quartering through the rolling waves. The chill lake breeze blew invigoratingly in his face and made him cheerful. Perhaps someday, he thought, he would come back here from Earth to fish for whatever native water-species there were in this lake. In spite of the gray, rolling water, the too-yellow sunlight and the different gray-greens of the tangled forest along the shore, the scene was strongly remindful of those few Canadian northwoods lakes that only existed on rare private estates back on Earth, nowadays . . .

He relaxed into thought, steering the canot with an automatic hand on the outboard tiller. Luckily Cohone in the flesh had turned out to be exactly as Harb had pictured him. Now, if Harb could only find a comparably useful individual in the Homskarter King Rajn, to whose court and wilderness city the canot was now headed ...

It should not be difficult. Thank the survey for that. Harb smiled slightly to himself. That was his difference from Cohone. The volunteer had studied the survey with an eye to advantaging the Homskarters. Harb had studied it with an eye to advantaging himself.

He had not, of course, told Cohone that whole truth. He looked down a little complacently now at the hard-muscled legs within the boots stretched out before him in the canot. He was young, in top physical shape, and thoroughly armed and prepared to deal with the courts of savages he was about to encounter. And that was another difference between him and Cohone. Cohone was trying to deal with a culture. Harb intended to deal with individuals.

... With the result that the Homskarters would make the cultural shift that the survey promised — bringing this world to a need for human aid and immigration. And bringing Harb the rewards obtained by one who added a world to the human community.

For World 49381D was in balance now — a balance that would need to be disturbed before any real progress could be made. It was a civilization that had its fingers stuck in the gears of the inexorably forward-turning wheel of progress toward a modern technological society. The present situation lay in stasis between the forest-country people and the people of the plains, on this

18

world's single great continental land mass sprawling like a skinny dragon three-quarters of the way around its globe.

The first human assumption had been that the already agricultural communities of the plains, with their primitive kingdoms, should be the ones humans might best infect with the concept of progress. But the survey had corrected that assumption.

The plains dwellers, with their crops, their caste system, and their mud-walled cities — their monarchs and merchant class — possessed a culture too fixed and brittle to adapt. The minds of the plains people were closed and they lacked cultural vigor.

No, said the survey, advancement on this particular world could only come from some vigorous, new culture which had no paralyzing old patterns to inhibit it from development. And the survey suggested that — working within the rules — the way to develop such a culture was to bring the hunting tribes and villages of the forests to a self-supporting agriculture. If this could be done, in time it would turn the forest warriors from raiders of the plains into a people concerned with their own land and development.

Freed of the pressure of yearly attack from the forest people, the plains civilization would grow weak and corrupt. Eventually it would either regress, or be swept away by the new civilization building in the woods to the north; and the forest people would begin to lead the long trek upward into a civilization comparable to that of modern humanity. At which point, hopefully, humanity would have acquired a new race of friends and partners. It was a careful plan, and a long one, looking some thousands of years into the planet's future.

Harb was more concerned with a plan that would show results in a matter of months. The basic idea of generating a developing society out of the forest people was sound. The trick of the survey plan, however — as Cohone had found — was to get these forest warriors to consider anything as demeaning as scratching in the dirt. The Homskarters, like all the forest peoples, lived mainly by hunting; but also by what food, primarily grain, they brought back from their annual raids on the plains. Particularly, they needed the grain to survive the months of the forest winters.

Each fall the Homskarters, like other forest tribes, gathered and pushed their canots through nearly a thousand miles of winding lakes and streams, to emerge with fire and sword upon the crops and walls of the plains' cities; and return with food and plunder to see them through another year in their forest fastnesses.

Sometimes, they were met by the more numerous, but less fierce, troops of the plains kingdoms and driven off; in which case there was starvation and disease among the forest dwellers that winter. More often, they conquered; and came back to spend the wintry months feasting and living high on the storable food, drink and other produce of the plains — eked out of the few primitive patches of root vegetables grown by the women they had left behind them.

And so the balance was held between plain and

forest. It was this balance Harb intended to upset. Not slowly, as recommended by the survey — not in Cohone's way — but suddenly and dramatically. He had spent the best part of the nine months since he had taken over this sector, first studying the worlds under him for one where such a dramatic change could be effected, then studying how the change might be brought about. Cohone, in fact, was not doing that much worse than the men on the other worlds of Harb's sector. But Cohone did have a world with a situation Harb could disrupt to his advantage.

It had taken some months of intensive work with records and computerized game plans, but Harb had eventually come up with what he wanted. Instead of a slow development of the forest people apart from the plains culture, why not make it possible for one of the forest leaders to become a Genghis Khan who could first take over control of all the forest tribes, then sweep down to conquer and occupy the plains?

The result would be a blending of the two cultures, with the forest people as warrior-aristocrats, and the plains people as a sub-caste of servants and slaves. From the brighter individuals of such a sub-caste, forbidden the warrior prides and occupations, could come artisans and scholars. And later on, when hybrid vigor began to manifest itself out of the crossbreeding of peoples, there would emerge true geniuses with intelligence and invention. Meanwhile, the quarrelsome warrior-aristocrats would have divided the plains into a number of competing kingdoms, so that individuals of

21

genius could find a number of different havens and a number of different patrons.

All that would be needed to get Harb his next promotion to Division Headquarters would be to show that this development had been fully begun by actions of his. Rajn, the so-called king of Cohone's Homskarters, was a leader of the sort needed, and his second-in-command was, according to Cohone's reports, no threat to such a plan. It needed only be put in Rajn's best interests to cultivate and harvest a surplus of grain — not merely enough for winter survival, but enough more for barter — to start the juggernaut of progress rolling.

Cohone could not do this, not only because of his attitude, but because he had come here with neither the proper plans nor equipment. Harb, on the other hand, had come with all these things. He patted the numerous, well-filled pockets of his jacket one by one, checking their contents.

CHAPTER THREE

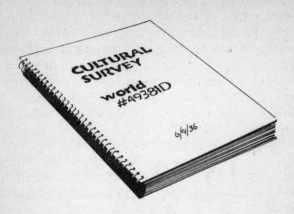

CULTURAL SURVEY
world #49381D

6/9/36.

Half an hour later brought him around a final headland into a wide and sheltered bay filled with canots ranging in size up to that of fifty-foot vessels with square sails. A wharf area was built out on pilings some distance from the shore; and behind the wharf on the mounting slopes of a hillside, was the palisade-enclosed cluster of wooden structures that was the "palace" of Rajn, King of the Homskarters, and the surrounding "city" of Homska. Altogether, they probably contained some twenty-five hundred native men, women, and children — which made this a forest metropolis.

Yet, thought Harb, steering in toward an inconspicuous corner of the wharf, it would not do to underrate Rajn on account of the small numbers of his people in this one settlement. When fall came, the total raiding force in his flotilla of canots, heading plainsward, would draw from the forest tribes of nearly a million square miles of surrounding territory; and his "army" would amount to as much as ten thousand backwoods fighters. Good fighters, every one of them — though, of course, there was no possibility of any one of them being as good as Harb himself. Not unless there was some individual equivalent of a superman among them.

He moored the canot by a wharf, the floor of which was four feet above his head. He jumped up, caught hold of the edge of the floor above him and swung himself up on to it. In spite of his attempt to come in as unobtrusively as possible, there was a small gathering already formed to examine him, his boots, helm, shield and weapons.

"Hey, Outlander!" said one of the foremost of these. "What happened to that hoe of yours? Looks like it got itself stuck in a sheath and turned into a sword. Is that really a blade you've got there? Let's see it."

The Homskarter was standing directly in front of Harb. It was a matter of pushing the broad-shouldered, hard-faced, hairy native in his cloth-wrapped body and limbs — red-wrapped arms, green-wrapped legs — out of his way, or walking around him. Harb stopped. He had no time to waste fighting with ordinary members of the native populace like this one.

"A sword it is," he answered smoothly in flawless Homskarter, "as you say — that used to be a hoe. I'm taking it up to King Rajn to show it to him. So maybe you'll pardon me, friend, if I don't stop to show it to you first. The king might take it amiss if it was you I stopped to show it to, before him."

Their eyes met. The eyes of the Homskarter, in his round, flat, snub-nosed face, were as gray as cold dishwater. Then the native stepped aside.

"Maybe you're right at that, Outlander," he said. "I wouldn't want to be the one to keep you from King Rajn. But maybe I'll see you again here, on your way home."

"That might be," said Harb, and went on through the city, up to the palace.

He attracted some attention going through the town and more so from the guards at the gate in the palisade surrounding the palace. But these, in spite of showing some amusement, made no attempt to bar his entry, but waved him on in. Harb had carefully studied the plan of the palace, and found his way without difficulty to the entrance of the largest building within the walls — the main hall of the king. He went up half a dozen steps to its wide doorway, passed a couple more guards, who also let him through, and walked into the main room of the hall.

It was a long chamber with tables down both sides at which warriors sat eating and drinking, rather in the manner of a perpetual picnic. At a small table crosswise to the others, and facing the entrance at the end of the room, sat a squarely-built Homskarter, not yet into middle age, with several others on either side of him. Even without his pre-study, Harb would have recognized the

center man as the most important individual in the room — Rajn, himself.

"Outlander!" shouted the Homskarter king, as Harb came forward between the flanking tables of the room. "What's happened to bring you here, away from your fields and weeding? And where'd you get the war tools?" He slapped the table before him and broke into the heavy coughing that was the equivalent of laughter among his race. "I know — you've had a plague of insects on your crops. And you come to ask my help!"

The whole hall broke out in coughing laughter. The king, Harb saw, was more jovial than drunk as yet, although it was mid-afternoon, and already the one heavy meal of the day would have been done — clearing the way for serious drinking and other sports such as story-telling, fighting, and brutal — if not lethal — practical jokes played on each other.

Harb continued walking forward until he was only half a dozen feet in front of the king's table.

"King," he said, calmly, in his accentless Homskarter. "I'm not surprised you don't recognize I'm not the outlander who tills his fields up the lake from here. To you Homskarters, I suppose, we all look alike. My name is not Cohone, like the outlander you know — but Harb. We're different."

King Rajn sobered. He leaned forward on one white cloth-wrapped elbow, and his long, gray-haired hand lay flat on the table in front of him. He looked at Harb with interest.

"Harb . . ." he repeated. It had been a fortunate coincidence that the name was one easy for the Homskarters to pronounce. Cohone was not.

Neither, for that matter was Harb's last name — Mallard. "Harb. . . . It's interesting. I've never seen one of the Others bearing weapons. I didn't think you outlanders had any."

"Some of us do," said Harb. "But if my weapons offend you, I'll gladly leave them outside this hall. Because I've come to ask a favor of you. I'd like, King Rajn, to go with you and your men on your raid this fall into the plains, in order to see for myself how the Homskarters handle such things. There's too little fighting to be had nowadays on our outlander worlds."

"I believe that, after seeing your fellow scratching like a woman in the dirt, up-lake," said Rajn. "But you aren't seriously claiming to be a fighter?"

"Some people might call me that," said Harb, mildly. "But if I might add to the favor I'm asking you, O King, I'd particularly appreciate it if you'd also extend me your royal protection while I'm with you. Just so none of your men'll challenge me to use these weapons of mine."

"Now, that's a strange request," broke out the Homskarter sitting next to the king. Like Rajn, he wore the royal cloth of white — on one arm only, instead of both arms, body, and legs. Harb identified him as Witta, Rajn's cousin and second-in-command, by vote of the Homskarter chieftains. He could not be sitting at the royal table unless he was blood-kin to the king — and only a close relative or full brother to Rajn would have dared to speak up unbidden like this. But a full brother would have had the right to wear two limbs white-wrapped instead of only one, as Rajn himself wore white on all four.

"Strange, indeed," said Rajn. "You want to come along with us to see fighting, but you ask me to protect you from any fighting with men of mine. Are you that afraid of the Homskarters, that you have to have my shield raised over you? If so, why should I take such a coward on my raid into the plains?"

"Why," answered Harb, mildly, "I don't think I'm any more afraid of your Homskarters than anyone else might be, whether he's a Homskarter himself or an outlander like me. It's true your warriors are all hard fighters; and I don't doubt there are some fearsome men among them. But it wasn't from fear, exactly, that I asked your protection. It's just because I'm a poet and a storyteller. And you ought to know that making proper poems and stories takes all of a man's attention — which can't be had if he's disturbed all the time by the exciting prospect of letting someone's blood."

For a moment the hall was silent. Then Rajn burst out into his coughing laughter, and the whole room resounded with it once more.

"By my sword!" Rajn shouted. "I've heard a lot of excuses for not fighting in my time, but I never heard an excuse like that! Poet and Outlander, you've got my protection! Provided you can make a poem or a story as well as you seem to think you can!"

"King!" shouted a voice from one of the long tables behind Harb. "Let me fight the outlander once first! After that, he can spend all his time making stories if he likes! A favor, King — a favor to match the outlander's favor! Let's see how he uses his weapons once, first."

"What if he went back to his own place and told how he was so clever he won a king's protection without ever proving himself?" interposed Witta.

Rajn's alien laughter slowed and stopped. He sat thinking for a while and Harb waited. Finally he nodded.

"Now, there's some sense in that, cousin," he said, and looked up at Harb. "Outlander, my protection's no light thing. You've got to prove yourself once anyway, to gain it. It's my decree you fight the man who just cried out for the right to fight you."

Harb shrugged.

"If it has to be that way, O King," he said. "Though I'd hoped not to have to reduce your following by even one worthy Homskarter warrior. But, as you say —"

He whirled. His ears had warned him just in time of the rustle of footfalls among the soft carpet of trash and bones on the floor behind him. He was able to swing about and get his shield up just in time to ward off the down-swing of a sword in the hand of a broad-shouldered Homskarter, who had crept up behind him.

Even prepared as he was with his special shield and other equipment, and trained by months of practice, Harb had not adequately anticipated the impact of that sword blow, delivered with all the native's strength. Literally, it drove Harb to his knees; and his shield-holding arm felt as if it had been broken. If he had been fighting with weapons actually equal to the Homskarters', the fight would have ended within seconds after that.

But the warrior's sword glanced off the metal

studs set around the rim of Harb's apparently wooden shield. The blade slipped downward, bit against the metal spike protruding from the center of Harb's shield, and broke off short — as is likely to happen when primitive iron comes hard enough against a sophisticated steel alloy. The Homskarter warrior paused to stare at his sword in amazement; and in that moment, Harb was able to regain both his senses and his feet. By the time someone at the nearby table had tossed the warrior another sword, Harb was ready for him.

He swung his own sword at the warrior's legs and the Homskarter dropped his shield to catch the blow. For a moment the upper part of his body was exposed and Harb, sighting through an apparently accidental notch in the top of his own shield, pressed a metal stud holding the handgrip of his own shield.

In the dimness of the hall, there were no eyes quick enough to see the tiny, dark metal sliver that flicked from the tiny hole in the point of Harb's shield-spike, to penetrate the heavy leather strips wrapping the upper chest of the warrior. With a shout, Harb charged into his opponent, clashing shield against shield.

The other reeled backward. Harb's sudden attack, their coming together, and the involuntary step backward the other was forced to take, all masked a sudden faltering of the native's sword arm, as the potent tranquilizer contained in the metal sliver began to act.

The Homskarter stumbled and sat down. Harb hewed downward with his sword at the unshielded head and the razor edge of his sophisticated steel-alloy blade sliced easily through the native iron of the helm of the other, hewing through skull and neck deep into the warrior's body.

A shout of amazement went up from the watchers at the tables in the room. Harb was forced to stand on the body to draw his sword out again. He wiped it, a little dramatically, on an edge of the dead Homskarter's kilt.

"That was a powerful blow, Outlander," said the king, as Harb turned once more to face him.

"Come and sit down here near the end of the long table on my right. If you can tell stories as well as you can fight, you're worthy of my protection, beyond doubt."

"I thank you, King," said Harb, moving over and taking the seat made for him on the long bench behind the table. "But I'd appreciate your excusing me from any story-telling, right now. As I said, the excitement of blood-letting's set my own blood buzzing in my head, and I can't properly remember the stories I'd like to tell you." He looked about the table. "Besides, even though I'm not hungry, the exercise —" he glanced at the dead body of his late opponent, now being dragged out of the hall by its heels, "has given me a thirst powerful enough to tell my grandchildren about."

The king coughed again with laughter, thumped the table, and shouted to the servants.

"Drink!" he roared. "Drink, for the fighting outlander!"

CHAPTER FOUR

A servant brought Harb a deep wooden bowl, filled with something over a quart of the flat, brown, ill-smelling liquid that was the local fermented grain beverage. Harb palmed into his mouth a tiny yellow pill which instantly overwhelmed his taste buds with a lemony flavor and poured half the bowl down his throat at once without either tasting or smelling what he swallowed. As the king coughed his approval, Harb emptied the bowl with another long series of swallows — and, as if this had signaled it, the day's serious drinking began.

It was obvious, before long, that the aim and interest of the Homskarters, including those at the king's table, was to see how much native beer this outlander could hold before the actually rather weak alcoholic content of it could put him under that table. He pretended to be unaware of their design, however, and drank on, parrying questions about himself and the type of outland he came from, in its difference from Cohone's, with the answer that he would tell them all at some future date when he had recovered from the excitement of his earlier duel.

In his turn, he studied those who drank at the king's table. There seemed to be a number of relatives besides Witta, including one brother barely old enough to bear weapons and too young to be a serious claimant to rule the Homskarters. Clearly Witta was undisputed second-in-command. But Harb noted with interest that, outside of the authority he bore, Witta seemed to show little talent for the position he held.

He was obviously a plain, dull, physically-minded warrior — probably of unusual strength, to judge by the width of his shoulders and the bulk of his body above the table. But though he showed none of the shrewd, if primitive, wit exhibited by the others at the royal table, all of the others, including the king himself, seemed to avoid making him the direct butt of any of their jokes and general horseplay.

Harb smiled to himself. The kingship among the Homskarters, his research had informed him, was theoretically hereditary — needing only to be ratified by a council of the chieftains. In practice, however, the survey had noted, inept heirs-apparent to the throne had a habit of dying off, or rejecting the crown, until the succession lighted on the most able of the royal family then of warrior age and capacity.

Thus in practice the king was actually chosen by the chieftains. So, also, was the second-in-command as the man next-best able to rule, although theoretically he should also be a member of the royal family. It would not be unusual under such conditions, however, noted the survey, for an unusually able claimant to the throne not only to get himself chosen king, but to control the choice of second so that the second should not pose the threat of usurpation that might well arise if the next-ablest man of the kingdom was continually sharing roof and board with the king himself.

Clearly, Rajn had chosen as harmless a second as he could. But, just as clearly, having chosen someone harmless, it was necessary to keep up appearances for the second-in-command. So, it was probably by will of the king that no one baited or teased Witta into any action that might betray his essential lack of personal authority and leadership.

Meanwhile, the drinking was beginning to tell on the rest of the Homskarters in the hall. One by one, they were succumbing to the native beer; they had compensated for its weakness by drinking tremendous amounts. Harb, although he was not in the least drunk, had filled and emptied himself half a dozen times over in order to keep up with them and show a proper capacity.

The only other individual in the hall not drunk, at least to a state of near-torpor, was the king. And this was another puzzle for Harb, since he had watched the king's bowl being refilled at least as often as his own. It was the same size bowl as everyone else had, though more ornately carved, and it was hard to see how the king had stood up to the amounts he must have swallowed from it.

Yet . . . there are limits to any animal capacity, human or alien, and there came a time when even the king, who had been blinking sleepily in Harb's direction for some time, dropped his head on his pillowing arms and did not stir again.

CHAPTER FIVE

Harb looked around him. As far as he could see, the hall was filled with unconscious warriors. Slowly, he got to his feet and picked his way up to the royal table. The king's drinking bowl was sitting, half-empty, by his elbow. Curiously, Harb picked it up, dumped out the liquid still in it, and felt inside it.

Sure enough, though it took a bit of fingering to make sure of it, the bowl had a curving false bottom, clever enough to trick the eye alone, even close up, but high enough in the bowl so that it held not more than half what other drinking containers held.

Harb nodded and set the bowl back down by the king's elbow. He went past the table back into the interior of the palace.

The layout inside was simple. Behind the royal tables were entrances to a huge kitchen, and what must be at least as large, if not larger, female quarters. The only other doorway opened on a flight of steep, circular stairs; and, climbing these, Harb at last came out on the top platform of the palace tower. He found himself on a circle perhaps twenty feet in diameter, with a breast-high wall, pierced with apertures, running all around it.

Harb walked over to the wall and leaned on it, breathing deep of the cold night air. Above, the stars twinkled. Below, the town was a dark splotch between the hillside and the lake — which was just now beginning to silver farther out, with a single, large moon rising over the hill behind the town.

"What do you see, Outlander?"

Harb whirled around. The voice had come from behind him, from the direction of the stairway. It had been thick, but thoroughly understandable; and as he turned, he saw the king walking slightly unsteadily but purposefully toward him. Immediately, Harb tensed. But then he saw that Rajn was unarmed, while Harb himself still had his sword at his belt — to say nothing of a dagger and several other, more inconspicuous and powerful modern weapons in his jacket pockets. Harb made himself relax. He leaned back once more with an elbow on the wall behind him.

"Nothing much, O King," he said. "Just the moonlight, the lake and your town."

"My town — yes." Rajn came unsteadily to the wall, leaned on it and turned toward Harb, bringing his dish-shaped face into the moonlight. The skin above his nose was deeply wrinkled in the native equivalent of a smile. "You hold your drink well, Outlander."

"Some might say so," answered Harb. The truth of the matter was, in fact, that he had not held it at all. Before coming to this world he had ingested a fungus-like strain of stomach bacteria that converted any alcohol he swallowed almost immediately to sugar. That particular digestive conversion, in fact, had been as nothing compared to the extended series of hypo-immunization shots he had taken in order to make it safe for him to ingest the native foods at all without massive and immediate allergic reactions.

"You're no small drinker yourself, King Rajn," Harb added.

"I've got a magic bowl," said the king, and coughed a short, drunken cough of laughter. "As perhaps you noticed, when you picked it up just now in the hall." He stared in the moonlight into Harb's face. "What brings you here, Outlander?"

"I told you, King."

"And I told you I had a magic bowl," replied Rajn, thickly. "No, Outlander, you're a warrior and a drinker, such as I've never seen; but you're here for some purpose you aren't telling me. And I don't intend you to leave until you do — " he broke off and coughed, as Harb stiffened instinctively. "You've got your sword, Outlander; and I've got nothing. Were you thinking of cutting my throat and getting away in the night? But the guards on the main door and the gate aren't drunk or asleep; and some hours back I sent word they weren't to let you out."

He peered at Harb.

"So, do you want to tell me now?" asked Rajn. "Or some time in the future — why you're here?"

"All right, King," said Harb. "As you see, I'm an outlander. Like the other outlander you know, I want to get your people started growing grain."

Rajn coughed, and the effort made him stagger.

"You've got a good feel for a joke, Outlander," he said, straightening precariously, and turning toward the stair. "We'll talk about this more tomorrow, you and I. Or the day after tomorrow . . . or the next . . ."

He reached the head of the stairs and Harb heard him stumbling down out of sight. But the king stumbled carefully, evidently, or else with the benefit of long practice on those stairs, for there was no sound of falling.

CHAPTER SIX

The next day, Harb put on a casual demonstration of how a wooden shield could be split and broken by a karate hand-blow. That evening, reciting a translation murmured into his ear by a small unit hidden there and in radio contact with a recorder computer in his right upper jacket pocket, he gave the assembled hall a poetic rendering of the legend of Beowulf.

The success was gratifying. For the first time, the Homskarter warriors began to gather around him and in the next few days that followed, he gradually became a celebrity second only to the king and Witta.

Meanwhile, Harb was observing these two royal individuals closely. The more he saw of Rajn, the more convinced he became that this was someone who in native intelligence and basic open-mindedness was far above the rest of his tribe. In contrast, the more he saw of Witta, the more Witta seemed to stand out as all that was representative of the brainless adherence to habit and custom among the Homskarters. If a contest had been held to choose a typical Homskarter, in terms of sword arm, physical appetite and refusal to consider anything outside the accepted pattern, Witta would have taken the prize.

Harb silently congratulated Rajn on picking such a second. If such a thing as respectability existed among the Homskarters, then Witta's endorsement of anything put the stamp of respectability upon it. A king who was more unorthodox in thought and action than most of his people needed someone like Witta around to assure the common herd that everything the king did was just as it should be.

With Witta himself, Harb made little headway. There was nothing particular about Harb to which Witta could object except that he was different. But that was enough. Harb's one or two attempts to scrape up an acquaintance with the second-in-command were rejected by Witta with dark suspicion.

Meanwhile, however, a wordless communication had been set up between Rajn and Harb. Both were clever individuals, and they began to draw closer to each other as the date of departure for the summer raiding approached. The night before leaving, they spoke frankly to each other once again. And on this occasion, too, the king chose the privacy of the tower for their conversation, just at twilight.

"Outlander," said Rajn. "The time has arrived for a meeting of minds between us. You come here to trade for something — I can smell the bargaining on your very breath. Now, the last time we spoke, you still insisted that what you want is for my warriors to give up the sword-trail and grow grain through the summer months. This is it, truly, what you have come for?"

"Not give up the sword-trail, exactly, King," said Harb. "But the grain can make you a mighty race."

Rajn came close to him and his flat face with its bridgeless nose looked grimly into Harb's. This time the king had come to the tower armed, and Harb became suddenly conscious that the small of his own back was pressing against the edge of the wall around the tower platform. As close as they were now, modernity of weapons was not the advantage it might have been otherwise. One shove from the king's powerful arms could tip Harb over backward to fall forty feet to the stones of the courtyard below.

"Farmer-work make you a mighty race?" Rajn snorted.

Harb gazed steadily into the gray eyes, deepset under the heavy brow ridge.

"King," he said slowly. "Take my sword and try it on something." Slowly, to remove any appearance of threat from the action, Harb drew his sword and handed it over, hilt foremost.

The king grasped the hilt, stepped back, and looked around. He took off his own helm, set it on a stack of stones piled up ready to be heaved down on the head of possible attackers of the tower, and lifted up Harb's sword.

He brought it down in a whistling cut. It clanged loudly, splitting the helm in two and cracking apart the rock just beneath. Rajn lifted up the sword and gazed at it in the last rays of the alien sun.

"Ah," he said softly, as if to himself, "a magic sword to match my bowl."

He did not offer to return the weapon.

"No, King," said Harb, almost as softly, "a magic hand. It has been said that whoever holds that blade shall have a magic hand for combat — provided only that the previous owner has worked certain necessary spells in making a free gift of the blade to the present owner. Otherwise a magic fire will slowly begin to consume the unprivileged hand that held the sword, until after some days there is nothing but a blackened stump."

Rajn stood quite still. Harb, watching closely, saw the king's hand loosen slightly on the hilt. This was not exactly surprising, for Harb had thumbed a small pressure point on the hilt in passing it over, and now a power-source linked to a strip of metal underneath the surface material of the hilt was slowly beginning to warm toward a temperature that would eventually make the hilt too hot to handle.

Absently, almost indifferently, after a moment, Rajn passed the sword back to Harb.

"Perhaps, before too long," he said, "you may be moved to make a proper gift of that weapon to me, Outlander. It would be a gift to bind the friendship between us."

"Assuredly, King," said Harb. "As soon as we have passed through the present spring and summer into next winter when the weather shall be cold enough to make safe the working of the

proper gift-giving spells. I take it, then, you'll be willing to let me accompany you to the plains after all — as a story-teller, of course, privileged to be free of such things as wielding a paddle or other duties which might interfere with my art as a story-teller."

"You will be welcome," said Rajn, almost dreamily. "But I wonder what benefits there are in your coming with us?"

"For King Rajn," said Harb, "there is, of course, the fact that I may soothe your cares by the occasional private telling of stories. Stories which may sometimes have knowledge in them you might find useful at the moment, in war and on the sword-trail."

Rajn looked at him with narrowed eyes.

"The outlander would give me advice?" he said.

"And what benefit is there in that for the outlander."

"The excitement of the sword-trail," said Harb, smoothly. "And of course, there is the matter that if Rajn becomes great in war and a great king, it is to my credit; both here and in that far-off place from where I come."

He hesitated slightly before adding a few more words. Ordinarily Rajn was too shrewd an individual to be taken in by flattery. But this was not so much flattery as a truth both recognized.

"It is my feeling that a king like Rajn is rare among rulers," he said. "And much may be done by him impossible to lesser men. I would be close to such a king."

Rajn coughed with humor.

"And it comes to me that if nothing else, you might sing me to sleep nights along the sword-trail, Outlander, with such pretty words." He turned away, adding over his shoulder, "You may come."

52

So the annual foray to the plains commenced.
The thousand-mile trip to the lower edge of the
forest country was a wild and thrilling adventure
even to Harb, who came from worlds that knew
star travel. The forest warriors moved in a pack of
high-sided, high-ended, fifty-foot-long cargo
canots, by lake and river and over forest portages
between these waterways, picking up more canots
and adventurers from other settlements that they
passed. By the time they paddled forth onto the
now-wide river that had carried them out of the

last of the shadows of the forest country into an open land of grassy meadows and rude, small farms, there were nearly eight thousand of the raiders.

Now they were approaching the arena of probable conquests. For some time the land had been flattening out around them. The rolling hills that had flanked them during the first few days after they emerged from the forest had begun to recede toward the horizon some time since; and now they looked out on flat territory stretching back from either bank of the river. It was territory mostly divided into farms or grazing areas, and with only an occasional clump of trees to break the monotony of level ground. Both land and air were dryer, and the temperature was warmer. The forest tribesmen threw off whatever they wore by way of clothing and went naked except for a minimum harness to which were slung their weapons and their most valuable smaller possessions. They sweated freely in the lowland heat and stank mightily. And they grumbled.

"How long, King?" A daring, if anonymous, voice called from one of the neighboring canots, one hot morning.

Rajn, who headed them all in authority over the chiefs and lords of the lesser forest tribes who had joined them along the way, pretended not to hear. The common warriors were growing impatient. Already they had passed by several of what could only be described as semi-prosperous villages, secured by palisades of vertical sharpened logs at least double the height of a warrior.

It was always a fine art for a leader like Rajn to know how long he could hold his raiders in check. Let them loose on upstream villages like these too early and casualties would diminish his forces for the richer targets farther downstream. Hold them in too long, and he could well have a mutiny on his hands and find both himself and his villagers slaughtered by those anxious to appoint a more aggressive warlord. Harb worried a little about Rajn holding back too long. If the mass of the raiders turned on the Homskarter king and his villagers, they would turn on the outlander who was of their party. And with all the sophistication of his secret weapons, not even he could deal with some seven thousand blood-hungry native fighting men all at once.

Rajn, however, was apparently reading signs in the behavior of his own people that Harb was not knowledgeable enough to perceive. Without warning, Rajn called his stentor. "Pass the word," he said. "We attack the next village."

The stentor, a Homskarter chosen for his powerful voice, shouted the decision to the immediately following canots, from where it was relayed to those further back. A roar of approval followed in its passage.

The canots erupted with a bustle of preparation. Bladed weapons were resharpened, and all other panoply of battle reoiled, restrung, or refurbished.

There was a whoop from the first canot. A new village had been sighted. The canots moved down-river steadily for it.

As they got closer, it seemed to Harb that some sense — it might in fact be the defenders' sense of smell — had warned them of what was coming toward them. As the canots approached the river-bank below the village, above the standing logs of the palisade, headgear and faces were thickly visible and busily in movement. Rajn stood in the prow of the foremost canot, talking loudly about the wealthiness of the particular village they were approaching, although Harb could see no significant differences between it and the villages they had bypassed until now.

The canots rushed toward the bank, the warriors in them unusually silent. Then, Rajn's leading canot drove its prow aground and those within it came boiling over the end of it. Leaping down to the muddy earth beneath they burst into a roar, which was echoed and amplified as other canots drove aground on either side of it and their occupants leaped to the land. Yelling, the forest warriors ran toward the village.

For a few literally frightening moments Harb, who had leaped unthinkingly with the others, thought that the rest of the raiders would carry him along in the press of their bodies into an assault upon the walls then and there — and it had not been his plan to get personally involved in any battle. However, just outside effective bow range from the wall facing them, the attackers slowed abruptly and came to a halt, falling silent again as they did so.

Now it was the villagers' turn to shout. A roar went up from behind the walls, as if the halting of the attack had been a victory won by the defenders. Weapons were skaken in the air above the palisade. When this at last died away, it was succeeded by a steady scattering of yells from both sides; and an intermittent exchange of stones and arrows began between attackers and defenders, none of which did any particular damage.

The forest warriors milled about, not so much

arguing with each other now as muttering to themselves, making grim motions at empty air and toward the enemy, and generally working themselves up toward an action fever.

Rajn had evidently been waiting for this particular moment. To the surprise and pleasure of Harb, who had been worrying that he might have badly overrated the Homskarter king, Rajn climbed up on a barrel-like container of drink and began to make a speech, calling the rest cowards in every fashion his language could provide, and lashing them with the extremes of insult and contempt.

The forest warriors gathered thickly about Rajn. They yelled back at him, waving weapons threateningly at first. But then, gradually, they fell silent. Ominously silent, thought Harb, who had prudently slipped back to the outskirts of the crowd. But Rajn continued to speak, still insulting the rest, but now mixing his epithets with references to the basic strength and fierceness of those he spoke to, subtly flattering them. They responded approvingly to this, and he slipped gradually into accusations and slanders against their opponents in the village. He worked them up to a wild roar of agreement; and he leaped from his platform, calling on all who were not the worst of cowards to follow him, and headed toward the gate.

The whole crowd streamed after him. He was a good ten yards in front of the rest as they crossed the midpoint of the distance between their camp and the palisade; but by the time they were almost to the wall he had allowed others to catch up and even to get somewhat ahead of him. Though he was not among the first to lift the scaling logs and climb them to the top of the wall, he was right behind those who were first.

The forest warriors did not yell, now. They saved their breath for fighting, ignored their companions who fell beside them under the hail of arrows and stones and swarmed up the scaling logs to the top of the wall. Soon there were a handful of them over the points of the logs and fighting toe to toe with villagers on the walkway just inside the top of the palisade.

All the while more of their companions were scrambling over the points of the logs to join them. Suddenly, the heavy gates in the palisade sagged open, whether broken through or unbarred from within by raiders who had gained the ground inside the village, Harb could not tell from his safe point in the rear of the attackers. Forest warriors shouted in exultation, streaming through the opening — and suddenly it was no longer a battle. The fighters around Harb were struggling now only to get into the village before those ahead of them had all the fun of slaughtering the defenseless and robbing the wealthy.

Harb let them go. No one on either side was paying any attention to him now. Sensibly it occurred to him that the forest warriors, drunk with victory, might well prove as dangerous to him inside the village walls as the original inhabitants might once have. He waited until the noise from inside the village had largely died down before taking a walk through the half-open gates.

There was not a great deal to see. The murder was just about over, but rape and a certain amount of amateur torture was still under way, the latter aimed at making sure that none of the villagers got away with keeping hidden possessions of value for wives or children sent off to safety before the raiders landed.

Harb was not the sort of man to be moved in any large, emotional way by the scenes in the village; but on the other hand they were hardly much in the way of entertainment. He turned about and went back out to the raiders' camp. There a victory party was already under way among those fortunate enough to have already found loot and returned with it. These were scarcely better company than their companions still in the village. Harb decided to retreat to one of the ships, made himself a warm bed of furs and settled down for the night. The noise on shore kept him awake for a while; then he fell into a sound slumber, rousing only briefly to find light reflections dancing on the inner ribs of the canot above his head, and discover that, by accident or design, the village was afire.

In the morning the only visible villagers were dead and most of the raiders were in a sour mood, inclined to grumble about their hangovers, the poverty of the village and the untrustworthy honesty of their fellows. The village itself was a blackened jumble of unidentifiable rubble. By midmorning, however, the canots were reloaded and stood off once more downstream.

They sailed past another two villages before Rajn judged it time to send the warriors once more after conquest and loot. Of the next five villages, they struck and conquered three, and soon they were attacking almost every village they passed.

They were into more southerly country now, where the spring was far advanced and the lands bordering the riverbanks were thickly settled. Now the raiders began making marches inland after looting the riverside villages, finding more remote little towns that were less well fortified and raiding these as well.

They brought their booty back on captured wagons pulled by the native draft animals, which looked something like zebras. In the process, Harb noticed that they gave a wide berth to the much larger population centers — small cities, with earth or stone walls up to thirty feet in height — obviously as much more able to defend themselves as they were much richer than the villages.

Harb smiled to himself. He and his equipment had, in assessing the situation here on 49381D, estimated with a high order of probability that the raiders would behave in just this manner. They had not come all this way into the plains to get themselves killed, even though it was obvious that pickings in such a city would be beyond comparison with the proceeds they could glean from the small villages they usually attacked. Harb chose a good hour of the evening when the sun was down and Rajn, at least, was not yet too drunk; and sought out the Homskarter ruler.

"King," Harb said, "it comes to my mind that with all your cares and duties you might be having some little trouble sleeping these nights. If you

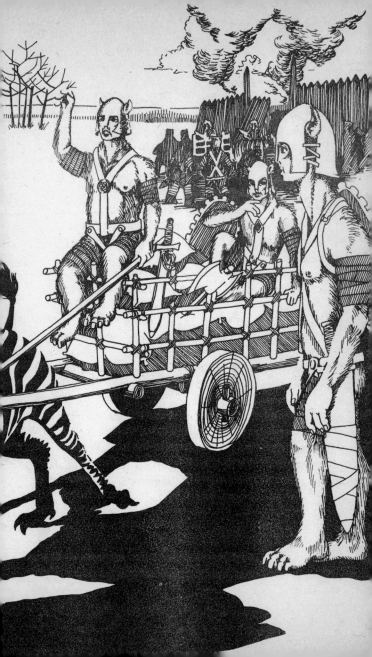

would care for a tale or two from me to soothe your weariness — a tale told privately, that is — it would be my honor to serve you."

"Well now, Outlander," said Rajn. He had been sitting before a fire, drinking with Witta and four of the lesser chiefs and his eyes glittered slightly under his brows as he looked up at the standing Harb. "It's strange you should mention that. It's true I've not had as much chance for sleeping as usual; and I owe it to the valuable warriors of our canots to keep myself in top fighting trim as an example to all. Suppose we take a skinful of this lowland drink back to my canot and you spin a tale or two there."

"Ho, Rajn!" said one of the lesser kings, who wore white wrappings on two of his arms and one leg. "Are the rest of us to miss out on these tales? A little fun might be good for all us leaders."

"Indeed — " Witta began sharply; then became silent as Rajn turned to look at him.

"But what if the tale-telling should make me wakeful instead?" said Rajn cheerfully, looking back at the chief who had spoken. "Brother swordsmen, let me try the outlander's yarning on myself first before I inflict it on the rest of you."

He got to his feet as he said the last few words.

"Come, Outlander," he added, and walked out of the firelight into the darkness before further argument could develop. Harb lost no time in following.

"Well," said Rajn, once he was settled on a pile of furs in the beached canot, with Harb seated opposite, "what tale had you in mind to tell me, Outlander?"

"Well, I've been thinking of a story about a king on the sword-trail who gave up the taking of small villages and instead took a walled city such as we passed earlier today on our way back to the river," answered Harb. "This city turned out to be so rich that the warriors he led had more wealth and grain than they could carry; and were able to go home early and spend the rest of the summer feasting and hunting."

Rajn spread the corners of his mouth in his race's equivalent of a yawn.

"I don't know that I care for impossible tales, Outlander," he said. "I like better those stories which could actually be."

"With eight thousand warriors," said Harb, "what is even a walled city?"

"Expensive, Outlander," Rajn's eyes glittered once more in the distant firelight coming over the side of the canot. "Far too expensive. What use the riches of a city, if only a handful are left to carry them home, and next summer only a slightly larger handful are waiting to take the sword-trail again?"

"But, King," said Harb, "in this story of mine, far more than a handful are left. Indeed, most of the warriors who attack live to return home rich."

"Ho? And how?" said Rajn.

"For that," said Harb, "I must tell you the tale. It seems this particular king had a friend on the sword-trail with him, an outlander of great strength, who could climb thirty feet of sheer stone wall with his fingernails and toenails . . ."

Harb proceeded to spin a yarn about a superman who could climb walls at night, silently, slay thirty city guardsmen without allowing any alarm to be given, and single-handedly open city gates so heavy that they normally required a pair of draft animals apiece to swing them apart, even after the massive bar that locked them had been lifted.

There was long moment of silence from Rajn after Harb had ended. Finally, he spoke.

"Would that such children's stories were possible," Rajn said. "But no king would risk his raiders on the chance of such an outlander being successful in such an attempt," He coughed laughter. "But do not think yourself unappreciated, Outlander. You have indeed made me sleepy."

"Risk?" said Harb. "What risk, King? If a king should march his warriors past such a city — again, just such a city as we saw earlier today in returning to our boats — on their way to take some other small village beyond such a city; and if it should happen that the warriors from the forest should camp overnight near the city, surely those within the city would not venture out?"

"Certainly they would not," said Rajn.

"Then," said Harb, "if in the middle of the night an outlander should come quietly to a king and tell him that the city gates were now open — or, better yet, a king should be in such position to see such gates open and rouse his men — what risk then?"

There was another long silence from Rajn.

"Now, that is indeed a thought," he said, at last. "I will sleep on your tale, Outlander."

Satisfied, Harb left him. The next morning, at

Rajn's orders, the raiders marched inland again to raid a village beyond the city.

That night found the raiders camped within half a mile of the city; and as soon as the dark was full, Harb slipped away from the others.

He crossed the open country between the camp and the city silently and without difficulty. Halting in the deep shadow at the bottom of the wall to the right of the city gates, he took off his shield.

He had brought sword and shield, not only because it would have seemed very strange indeed to any native to see him adventuring without it, but for more personally important reasons. Beneath its wooden covering, the incredibly tough alloy of which the shield was constructed was honeycombed with small compartments. Harb opened one of these now and took out a small, pistol-like device.

Balancing it in one hand, he touched another trigger point on his helmet that slipped heat-sensing night-glasses down over his eyes. Looking along the top of the wall on either side of the gate with them, he picked out on each side the auras of three warm and living bodies, creating slight clouds above the stone.

He moved away from the gate down the wall to his right until he was a safe distance from the auras, then stopped and fired the pistol-like device upward. A tiny projectile pulling a wire behind it leaped from the gun-muzzle to the top of the wall, and buried itself deep in the stone there. The impact made only the faintest of sounds. Harb grasped the wire where it emerged from the pistol muzzle and hooked it back through a small wheel-point in the middle of the device. Then, taking hold with each hand on a half of the pistol-shape, he prepared to go up the wall — his shield hanging at his back and the scabbard of his sword tied to his left leg.

But he hesitated. Abruptly, he became aware that his heart was pounding fast within him — so fast and hard he could feel it thudding heavily inside his chest wall. It was true enough that he was carrying sophisticated equipment that should make the execution of what he had set out to do a sort of child's play.

But what if something went wrong? What if something unexpected should crop up, something outside his planning?

He hesitated. It was still possible for him to turn around and go back to the camp. Rajn would laugh at him secretly when morning came without anything happening. But the king was too shrewd to do more than that, or in any way risk losing Harb, as long as there were things yet to be discovered or gained from the outlander. And given time perhaps Harb could come up with another, personally safer, way to insure that the raiders took a city like this.

But the moment of doubt and queasiness passed. Harb braced himself, pressed a button on the wire-gun, and a tiny but powerful winch inside it began to reel back into the muzzle the wire it had spat out, lifting gun and Harb to the missile-head buried in the stone at the top of the wall.

Harb reached the top, clung with one hand to the wire-pistol while he got a grip with the other on the stone edge, then climbed up over the parapet and down on to the sentry walkway behind it. He crouched there.

Ahead, his heat-sensing glasses now picked out sharply the heat images of the three sentries on this side of the gate. Predictably, and undoubtedly against orders, they were all clustered near the gate-end of the walkway, talking to each other.

They were about seventy feet from Harb, but with the heat-sensing glasses to guide his aim, this distance was no problem. He detached the wire-end from its half-buried missile, put that device away and took from his shield a small handgun. He sighted it, and fired. Tiny, rocket-shaped projectiles leaped silently from its muzzle to bury themselves deep in the bodies of the three sentries. The three heat-auras slumped one by one to the walkway and lay unmoving.

Harb walked up to the sentries and found them all dead. He cut their throats for appearances' sake and then turned his attention to the ground within the gate.

Down there his glasses showed twelve more auras. Silently, one by one, he shot these also, and saw them slump to the ground. Then he went softly to the stone stairs leading up to the walkway on the far side. Here also, the unsuspecting sentries were clumped together talking. He fired, saw them drop, and climbed the stairs to cut their throats. Then he went back down to the ground level, and gave visible death wounds to all the sentries he had slain there. Finally he turned his attention to the gate.

Within minutes, he had used the wire-gun to cut through the massive wooden bar, and then

winch open the heavy gate. As soon as the aperture was big enough to let Harb's body through, he squeezed through into the open air beyond, feeling a vast relief.

"Ho! Who're you? What're you doing — "

The voice exploded behind him. He turned to see an armed figure squeezing through the crack in the gates — behind him.

There was no time to think. He had been spotted, and the alarm would now be raised. It had all been for nothing unless he could get Rajn back here before the city people found some way of rebarring the gate. Harb turned and ran, cursing his fate. The half-mile to the camp was no short run to make, loaded as he was with shield and sword.

The shield, at least, could be picked up later. He threw it away. And then, just at that moment he heard the thud of running feet, not from behind but ahead of him. Fear took him by the throat. There must have been sentries outside the village walls as well as inside. Now he was trapped between the outside sentries and the individual behind who had surprised him; and he had nothing left but his sword, and what was in his pockets. These were vastly superior weapons to any his opponents would be carrying; but the really heavy artillery, so to speak, that he possessed were all in his shield, lost somewhere in darkness behind him.

A clamp seemed to close on his throat. Panting, he stopped and yanked out his sword.

Without warning the running feet before him were upon him. Their bodies surrounded him —

and he almost sobbed with relief. Even in this semi-darkness he recognized Rajn and a body of the forest warriors.

They rushed past him toward the opening in the gate, all but Rajn, who stopped briefly to peer into his face in the dimness.

"Did you think I wouldn't follow you closely this night, Outlander?" said Rajn. He coughed his humor and went off at a run after his warriors, who were already pushing through the partially open gate.

Harb turned back hastily to hunt for his shield and located it just as the light thunder of a much greater number of running feet struck his ear. Rajn must already have sent a runner back to rouse the camp. Yells and sounds of fighting were already beginning to come from within the gates, and as Harb looked, the gate-half he had pulled ajar with the wire-gun swayed and squealed further open to make a gap half a dozen men could enter abreast.

Prudently, Harb ran to one side and watched the dark, heavy mass of the raiders, beginning to shout and howl now that there was no more reason for silence, pour past him into the city. An unbroken river of fighters was coming from the camp. No doubt in another half hour every forest warrior would be within the city. Harb took himself apart to wait for dawn and what it might show.

What it showed was a captured city completely in the hands of forest warriors, except for a single large building that seemed to be a sort of meeting-house or town hall in the center of the city. This building was apparently crammed with several hundred of the city inhabitants; and these were only alive when the rest of the original populace lay dead, because the forest warriors had literally grown weary of killing.

Harb went in search of Rajn. He found the Homskarter king, one of a drunken party with Witta and the other lesser chiefs. All were apparently asleep or unconscious in a shop on the same square that held the large building enclosing the remaining living city people. For a moment, Harb thought that Rajn had passed-out with the rest; but as he came close the king opened his eyes and looked at Harb with a gaze that did not show drunken at all.

"Outlander . . ." he said loudly and thickly. "Help me outside . . . I need some air . . ."

Harb came forward and gave the king an arm. Rajn pulled himself to his feet and leaned heavily on Harb as Harb helped him out into the silent square. Once beyond view from the doorway, however, Rajn shook himself free of Harb's arm and walked with perfect balance around the corner of the building they had just left into a little blind alley where they were out of sight of anyone else.

"Well, Outlander," he said, turning to face Harb. "I've been waiting for you to show up. Name your price."

"Price?" echoed Harb.

Rajn's eyes slitted.

"We each know the other to be no fool, Outlander," he said. "Don't waste my time. You gave us an entrance to this city with an eye to your own profit in some way. I'd be no king but a fool to believe otherwise. Now I ask you what that price is."

Harb shrugged.

"I've told you, King," he said, "what's to your benefit is also to mine. Now you have all the loot and food your warriors can carry. Return home with it and be happy."

"Happy?" Rajn coughed. "There is more than happiness in this, Outlander."

"Why should there be?" said Harb. "I can even tell you how to take home more than you now think you can carry."

Rajn looked at him.

"Say on," said the king.

"You have lost a few of those you started with," said Harb. "On the empty benches among your canots, you could carry at least two or three hundred other paddlers."

He paused.

"Say on, I said," repeated Rajn.

"If you'd take a couple of hundred or so stout men and women from that building, there," Harb waved in the direction of the meeting-house where the city inhabitants were waiting their doom, "they could learn to paddle, portage and carry for you. The canots could be more heavily loaded with grain, weapons and other things of worth from this city."

Rajn grunted a negative.

"Those who still live must be sacrificed to the Gods who smiled on us and let us capture this city," he said. He shot an ironic glance at Harb. "Or so my warriors would say if I should suggest what you suggest."

"What's wrong with taking the prisoners home and sacrificing them there?"

"Home? Take who home? What — who home?"

grunted another voice and Witta reeled into sight around the corner of the building.

"Cousin," said Rajn, softly, "the outlander is pleasuring me with one of his tales."

"Outlander!" The hair on Witta's shoulders erected itself in drunken rage. "Flay and gut all Outlanders — "

His voice caught in his throat, his shoulder hairs wilted. For all his careful study of the natives of this planet and the Homskarters in particular, Harb was never sure of reading their expressions. But it seemed to him that shock and fear — almost a superstitious fear — at what he had just said, was visible for a moment on Witta's face and body.

The second-in-command of the Homskarters turned and staggered back around the corner of the cul-de-sac, out of sight.

"You didn't answer me, King," said Harb, in the silence that followed. "What's wrong with taking the prisoners home and sacrificing them there?"

"What, indeed?" said Rajn agreeably. "A wise thought, Outlander."

"Good," said Harb, relieved. "You won't regret going home this early. In fact, I'll promise you that this is your first step to more than you've ever dreamed of having."

"All things wait to be born," said Rajn. He turned away and went out of the blind alley, rediscovering his drunken stagger as he passed the corner of the building, around which Witta had vanished a moment before.

CHAPTER SEVEN

Harb headed back out of the city and found himself a safe spot in the center cargo area of Rajn's boat, to catch up on the sleep he had lost. Nothing was absolutely sure with the natives of this world; but the overwhelming odds were that the sanctity of a king's craft, plus his own reputation, would make him fairly safe from anyone who might consider sneaking aboard with robbery or murder in mind. Just to be on the safe side, however, he set his metal detector to wake him if anything metallic should be brought within two meters of him.

A little later he woke to realize that the boat was being moved; but since there was no reason to suspect any danger to him in that, he merely went back to sleep again. He was more tired than he had thought and he slept heavily.

When he did wake, it was to the boat-sway and noises that signalled that they were once more travelling. It was late afternoon when he sat up to glance about him; and he could see that the whole expedition was afloat, moving together.

He felt a surge of pleased surprise. Rajn had evidently lost no time in turning back toward the forests. Not only that — apparently he had experienced no deep problems in talking the other petty kings and chieftains into turning back with him. Harb sat up further and looked around for the city-dwellers that were being brought back as slaves. There were none in this boat, but that was not surprising, since Rajn's was the command craft and any casualties among its crew had been promptly replaced from other Homskarter canots as soon as vacancies appeared.

But, when Harb looked over at the nearby craft, he saw no city-slaves aboard them. Even taking into account the high sides of the canots, the broader-faced, shorter-haired plains dwellers would have been easily identifiable.

Rajn certainly would not have been foolish enough to turn back without taking slaves and grain with him? Harb felt a sudden uneasy emptiness in him. Going back without slaves and grain made no sense . . .

He checked the thought suddenly, struck by a suspicion.

Getting up, he moved to the nearest side of the canot. Here, in the cargo-carrying midsection of the boat, there were no paddlers and he could literally hang over the side. It took a moment or two of checking the river surface for bits of floating debris far enough from the canots so that the drift of such flotsam was not affected by the swirling of the paddles — but then he saw clearly what he had feared. The canots were moving with, not against, the current, continuing downstream further into the plains country.

The back of Harb's neck went cold and his mouth went dry. He swallowed his anger, which would do him no good now. When he had last spoken to Rajn, the king had promised a return to the forests. . . .

Or had he?

Harb was wide awake now and his mind galloped. Like all the rest of his people, the Homskarter king was adept at saying something that sounded like one thing but was actually something else. What had been Rajn's exact words when Harb had pressed him to know what was wrong with taking the slaves and grain and heading home?

"What, indeed?" Rajn had said.

Now that the words were reechoing in his head, Harb could recognize how far from an unconditional agreement to his plan they had been. With no trouble now, he understood. By Homskarter reasoning, Rajn would be a fool to turn back home just when he had discovered how useful Harb could be in opening up walled cities. Grain and slaves were useful things, something Rajn could appreciate during the long winter months. But right now, like all the other raiders, what would be glittering much more attractively in his imagination would be the metal implements, the weapons, cloths and all other such booty to be acquired from the more sophisticated civilizations of the plains cities.

It would be only when he had his fill of these other, more luxurious items, that Rajn would turn back. Harb swore at himself. He should have realized that fact.

Now, he gnawed his lip. The question was how much booty Rajn would want to win before he could be talked into turning back — or whether there might be a way of tricking him to forgoing some share of it. Harb left the side of the boat, moved back to its center and drank from one of the kegs of plains ale that had been brought aboard from the last conquest. It was not the best of drinks, even with his lemon-taste pills, but it washed away the sleep-dryness from his mouth. Then he moved on up to the sterncastle platform, where Rajn rested, momentarily free of companions and sprawled out on a pile of the green and grey-striped cloth that was also part of the late city's loot.

"King," said Harb, from the foot of the three steps leading to the platform, "are you in a mood to talk to an outlander?"

"Well now," said Rajn, peering down at him over the edge of the royal drinking bowl, "you judge my mood very well. Come and talk to me, then."

Harb mounted the platform and sat down crosslegged on it, a little off the pile of cloths on which Rajn lay.

"I see we are once more on the path of conquest, King," he said.

"I have always said, Outlander," replied Rajn, "that your vision was of the best — considering what you are and where you come from, of course."

"Does the King have in mind the next place we will conquer?"

"Perhaps . . ." said Rajn. He drank from the bowl, watching Harb as he did so. "Have you ever seen a city built on a mountain, outlander?"

"In other places, I have indeed seen cities built alone in high places," said Harb, cautiously. "Whether that's what Rajn the King means, of course, I can't say. What I've seen could be very like — and then it could be a great deal different."

"It's probably different, Outlander," said Rajn. "Still, someone like yourself will probably come to understand it well enough. This is a city built on a steep mountain that rises from the plains at a point where this and another river come together, so protecting the mountain on two sides. A very steep mountain it is, and a very rich city — but with very high walls and more rocks than are necessary to roll down the sides of the mountain at anyone attacking it."

"I . . . see," said Harb.

"But a wise outlander like yourself will undoubtedly have a plan for avoiding such rocks and taking the city anyway," Rajn said. "There would certainly be no doubt about that, either. Would there?"

Harb had to think quickly.

"No, King," he said. "Of course not. Naturally, I'd have to study this high city first, so that I could understand the differences between it and the sort of high cities I've been used to."

"Naturally," said Rajn. "I would expect no less. By all means take half a day, or even more, to study if you wish."

Harb shook his head. He had reached a point where it would be wise to dig in his heels a bit.

"The small skills and magic I possess," he said, "would, I'm afraid, never be able to bridge such a wisdom-gap in half a day. An eight-day, possibly — "

"An eight-day, Outlander," said Rajn, "is too long."

Harb shook his head again.

"I would hope it would take less than a week, of course," he said, "but I would not want, either, to promise the king of the Homskarters something that would need several more days than I had promised. Perhaps I might do this in less than a week, if I was very lucky, but to promise anything less than six or seven days — "

"One day at the outside, Outlander," said Rajn.

"What can I say?" replied Harb. "I can *tell* the king one day if he wishes to hear that, but certainly it can't be done in that short a time. Six days would be the absolute least amount of time to discover a way to take such a city."

"Two days. That's the most these fighting men will wait."

"I understand," said Harb — and in fact he did. To hold an expedition like this one idle for more than two days, with a prize like a wealthy city in plain sight, would be for Rajn to seriously risk his authority. "But there's no need for them to do nothing but wait while I work out a way to get past the city walls. There are some things that I have to do in any case; and other things, which if done, will help me to reach my own answers much more quickly than I would if I didn't do them. For one thing, I need to see this city defending itself so that I can best understand how it does so. I have to see at least one attack on it — and who knows, such an attack might even succeed, thereby saving a very great deal of time and trouble."

"True," said Rajn. He drank. "There is always that."

"To be really certain, however," said Harb, "I should really see two attacks — "

"Outlander," said Rajn. He lowered his head and his voice barely reached the ears of Harb alone. "You'll see two attacks that fail to take this city only if I am convinced beyond all doubt that in no way can a third attack fail to win it easily. Also, four days is all the time you will have — and if you're wise you'll count on only the first three of that four, if you have hopes on yourself, or I, or any of us from Homska, seeing sunset of that fourth day after two failed attacks."

Harb met the other's eyes. They were direct and unyielding.

"I understand, king," he said. "How soon might we be reaching this city and the other river?"

"Two days."

"I understand," said Harb. "I promise you, therefore, this city in four days."

"And I accept your promise, Outlander," said Rajn. "Now, I'm tired of talking."

Harb went back to the cargo area, lay down again, and closed his eyes in a pretense of sleeping. How he would go about getting into a fortified city on a mountain, he had no idea. But he had been in no position to plead an inability to do so.

Behind closed eyelids, now, he put his mind to work, and continued to keep it at work as they continued downriver and pulled ashore at sunset to set up cooking fires and what passed among the forest dwellers as an overnight camp. Chiefly, this meant some hide tents for the kings and chieftains, and a few feet of open ground with a fur or two to wrap around each of those who were both sober and careful. Most of the expedition simply ate and drank themselves insensible, and slumbered uncovered where they fell.

Rajn chose to sleep on board his craft. That put it off limits to everyone else, including Harb. So Harb went off away from the encampment to build himself a small security nest in a patch of tall grass.

He was busy using his mind and memory. Before he had come, in the six months in which he had prepared for this trip, he had intensively studied a number of very good photos of the plains areas usually covered by the Homskarters and their fellow forest raiders on their summer forays. He had, in effect, memorized the territory of their possible routes on this expedition and now that memorization paid off.

Clear to his mind's eye came a picture of the city Rajn was talking about. It stood, as the king had said, at the confluence of the river they were now on and another equally as large that flowed into it almost at a right angle. The city was a high-walled, well-fortified place, certainly, but — Harb remembered now — it was somewhat of an exaggeration to say that it was sited on a mountain. Actually it occupied the top of a limestone bluff between the two rivers at the point where they joined — a limestone bluff that had had its further approach eroded away by spring flooding and some centuries of traffic, so that the city was actually perched on a steep-sided hill.

The realities of the situation, however, did not make easy the task of sacking such a city with the kind of troops available to Rajn and no seige artillery. The north and west slopes to the city, except for the switchback road leading up to its main gates, were bristling with stones and boulders of all sizes. Some of these had perhaps weathered out of the limestone, but a good number, at least on the upper slopes, had obviously been deliberately brought in and lined up so that they could be rolled down on attackers. At first glance it looked like the kind of stronghold that it would require modern human heavy weapons to take.

Bedded down in his grass nest, with his detectors set to warn him of any unexpected approach, Harb vigorously rejected the idea that the place should be so unconquerable. Anyway this primitive should not offer that much of a problem to someone like himself.

Of course it should. Still . . . he fell asleep at last that night, without having come up with the answer he so confidently expected.

CHAPTER EIGHT

As Rajn had promised, it was not until the second day after leaving the city they had last taken that they came to the one on the mountain. They had moved from a very flat plains area gradually into one in which the terrain was more rolling, so that the crests of soft, tan-colored hillsides on either side of the river made for close horizons. So it was that they came on the high city all at once. One moment it was not visible, and then the river made a turn around the flank of one of the soft land-rises to their left, and they caught sight of the city, clear and plain, though still some distance off, in the bright, early afternoon sunlight.

At first sight, to Harb at least, the city was unimpressive. In spite of himself, in spite of the satellite pictures he had seen of it, he had been expecting something castellated and forbidding; and with the problem of entering it continuing to go unsolved, his mental image had grown emotionally until he had been envisioning something like the Krak des Chevaliers, the ancient fortress built by the Knights Hospitallers of St. John back on Earth in Syria. But what appeared, when he at last saw it, seemed nothing more than an untidy collection of mud-brick buildings crowning a hill, with a few stone edifices in the center of them, and a defensive wall wandering almost aimlessly about the slopes below. It was a wall that from this distance looked low enough to be stepped over by a long-legged adult.

A second and longer look revised Harb's opinion. In full view of Rajn and the others he dared not use the monocular he had hidden in his shield, to get a closer view, but even from where they viewed it, he was able to realize that the buildings he was looking at made up a population center at least twice the size of the walled city they had taken earlier. Also, the reason that the wall had seemed to wander crazily was actually because it was built to take advantage of natural small cliffs and vertical drops upon the hillside, which in many cases effectively doubled its height. Finally, the diminishing effect of distance had to be allowed for. The wall, he decided finally, must average well over two meters, and might well average three. Moreover, it seemed in very good repair.

If Harb had lacked a certain amount of proper awe at first sight of the city, however, the forest natives surrounding him more than made up for it

with their own reaction. A silence and motion-lessness fell over the normally noisy canots as the city was revealed to them by the bend in the river, a silence that lasted until the sudden cessation of paddling began to result in canots drifting into each other at the whim of the river current.

Collisions sparked arguments. Arguments broke the spell and paddles were dug in briskly once more. So they came to the river landing below the landward side of the hill; and the raiders boiled out to crowd that portion of the shore looking up the approach road to the city gates, which were already, prudently, closed.

It was a measure of the reaction among the forest natives at the sight of the high city that they did not immediately go into their first rush against the objective as was usual with them on landing from their ships. Instead they stood around, talk-ing among themselves, until Rajn mounted a keg carried ashore for that purpose and made a long speech.

He began by painting an impressive picture of the might and wealth of the high city, drifted gradually into implying all sorts of compliments to the bravery of the expedition's warriors for even considering an attack on it, and from there went on to explain that the city was sadly fallen away from its former power and actually was overripe for sacking — provided, of course, the sacking was attempted by heroes like those he now spoke to. Finally, he wound up by painting a picture of the valuables to be found in this formerly invincible stronghold. The forest natives began to yell with excitement and wave weapons in the air.

Primitive the Homskarter king might be by human standards; but his speechmaking was effective. He built his audience to a high pitch of excitement and then capped it by suggesting that, since it was too late in the day to mount a serious attack on the city, they might nonetheless pretend to make an attack, so as to thoroughly frighten the defenders and take the heart out of them for the real assault which would be coming up tomorrow.

The warriors howled and leaped about. Then, in an explosion of action, the customary first false rush erupted and was carried through with all the more gusto in that the falseness of it had been acknowledged and agreed upon beforehand. The invaders swarmed up to within an axe-throw of the wall. There was a great deal of shouting and threatening both on their part and on the part of the defenders. The city people, however, proved to be better supplied and more accurate with their throwing spears than the plains people customarily were; and after some minutes the forest natives withdrew to the edge of the river, and made ready to settle themselves for the night.

Rajn immediately sent parties out to scour the countryside for local natives who could be questioned about the defensive arrangements and the number of fighters to be encountered within the city walls. Other groups were detailed to build ladders and men were sent out to find and bring back a tree trunk large enough to make a useful battering ram against the city gates. Meanwhile, the rank and file of the forest natives were busy sharpening their weapons, and discussing the situation. An unusual air of seriousness and determination pervaded the camp.

Harb made a solitary tour completely around the hill to examine the city from all sides. This was not difficult to do on the landward side, but on the side that faced the place where the two rivers joined, the slope of the hill came steeply down to meet the water and he was forced to scramble along on his hands and knees in places, rather than risk sliding down into the water. He discovered little, however, except the impracticality of using the river confluence side as a slope up which an assault might be made. He was in a bad humor by the time he reached the more or less level ground facing on the other stream, and his mind was made up. The only solution was to divert the expedition from this unconquerable community to a more achievable goal.

He had already given this some thought in the boat coming down, while he had been mentally reviewing the surrounding territory. Now he hunted up a dry patch of brush in which to make his personal bivouac and there, in privacy, activated the small library screen that was hidden under a plate of the shield's inner face.

The light of the day was already fading toward twilight and the screen had been necessarily miniaturized to fit in with all the other equipment he had wanted to hide in the shield; so he was forced to peer closely to make out details on the maps and satellite photos the screen produced for him. But he found that his personal memory had been reliable. About five days upstream on the river they had just joined, it found its source in a very large lake indeed. Out of sight of the shores of that lake, in its center, were a cluster of islands on which a separate kingdom had evolved, protected by the watery barrier around it, but with no other natural defenses.

The islanders, according to the satellite survey, were a people who made their living in boats and who over the years, off the main raiding routes as they were, had gone untouched for some centuries. Their accumulation of riches, accordingly, should make even those of this high city look small and mean by comparison; and their unguarded islands should be vulnerable to the canot-borne forest raiders as they had never been to the armed forces of the other plains kingdoms.

Harb covered the screen on his shield and went to seek a moment alone with Rajn, to suggest a change of target for the expedition. But Rajn's eyes looked coldly at him.

"Ill news," said the king, "ill news is even a worse friend when it comes untimely."

The light from a nearby cooking fire — for the sun was down now and only a last flush of twilight stained the western sky — made Rajn's face look shifting and bestial.

"But, king," said Harb, as winningly as he could, "only five days away — rich islands with no wall about them, and with no warriors accustomed, as these city warriors must be, to making a strong defense — "

"A hungry man does not easily give up meat in hand on merely the promise of more meat five days hence," said Rajn. "Outlander, you are somewhat late with this sort of news. I would not try to turn these fighters from this city now, even if that was what I wished myself."

He swung about and walked off a few steps, then paused and turned back.

"I'll look to hear a story of another sort from you by tomorrow noon," he said, slowly. "A story that will please me better."

He turned away again. This time he kept going. Looking after the broad back and heavy shoulders, silhouetted against the last light of the sky, Harb felt a wary coldness. He might have hoped to bluff out the other forest natives if they should threaten to turn on him. But Rajn was too intelligent to risk bluffing. Enough of the primitive Homskarter weapons could overwhelm everything that Harb was carrying — and Harb suspected that Rajn had guessed this.

The next day the assault went forward as soon as the sun was halfway up the sky and the last of the overnight mists from the river had cleared off the main slope. It was a serious and hard-pressed attack — even Harb was impressed by its earnestness. The battering ram reached the gates and even managed to split one of them, although the locks and hinges held. Several of the ladders that had been built were brought into position against the walls; and some of the attackers achieved the top of the walls, but were either killed or thrown off and the ladders pushed down. By noon, the attack was over. The forest natives retreated down the slope.

Tempers, Harb knew, would be short among the unsuccessful raiders and probably Rajn's as well. Harb made it a point to stay well clear of the expedition's members as they settled down to

drown their disappointment in drinking and re-
criminations. For something to do, he went out to
make another surveying circuit of the hill; and
found, to his pleasure, that the opposite side of it
where the two rivers came together was now
shadowed from the now hot sun by the height of
the hill itself. The combination of shade and the
cooling gurgling water only a dozen feet away
from him, was pleasant. Harb sat down to enjoy
the unexpected comfort.

The continuous sound of the water finally reminded him that he was thirsty. He got up and
went to kneel on the bank and dip up water in his
cupped hand to drink. The water was fresh and
cool — and as he was drinking his third handful,
illumination suddenly struck, so that he stood
poised, the ignored water spilling forgotten, trick-
ling down his forearm into his sleeve.

Of course, he told himself, grimly! He had not
been using basic common sense.

The high city was obviously designed for defense against just such seiges as this. Along with
the well-made wall and gates and the armed and
ready condition of the populace, it must have re-
serves of food — and a water supply within the
walls, so that the inhabitants could not be forced
to surrender as a result of their own thirst. Ordinarily, that would mean wells had been dug
within the walls. But wells could not be the solution here. The city on the hilltop was several
hundred feet above the water table indicated by
the two rivers here, and a second's thought by
Harb's educated and civilized mind should have
been enough to point up the fact that a society at

this historical level would not yet have the skills to dig wells over two hundred feet deep, without the sides collapsing in on them. Nor could they draw up from such wells enough water to sustain a whole city.

Harb cursed himself for an idiot.

Of course, he should have seen the obvious answer. The basic rock of the hill was limestone. Limestone soft enough to be carved with iron tools, and which, as well, was prone to be cut and leached away by natural and surface and other waters, forming caves. There absolutely must be an interior set of caves, whether natural or improvised by the city dwellers, that led down inside the hill to the level of these rivers. That had to be the answer to where they were getting their drinking water, safely and out of sight of any attackers.

And if there was indeed such a series of interior caves or vertical tunnels down to the river level, it could well be that there would be access to them underwater, here, at the foot of the hill.

Seconds later, Harb had cut a sapling from the river's edge and was probing the depth of the water just at the bank. The normally shallow rivers that joined here had scoured out a greater depth at their point of meeting. But just at the bank, where the face of the hill continued down underwater, Harb was overjoyed to discover depths of no more than two to three meters before the steep slope of the immediate underwater changed to a more leisurely descent to the greater depths farther out in the confluence.

He peered down through the water. It was not clear enough for him to see the further bottom; but underwater visibility should be good enough for his needs. He stripped off his clothes and began an underwater search of the hill-face just below the water surface.

The water felt icy cold at first touch, after the hot air, but it was actually not that bad, and he adjusted to it. Less than two hours later, with only three pauses to rest and warm himself on the bank above, he had located an opening a meter and a half down in the underwater bank, big enough for him to swim into. He came back up to his clothes and equipment to get a small fusion torch that would burn underwater.

The torch was not ideally designed to be used as a source of illumination in the below surface dimness; but it would do. He dived back down with it and by its light examined the opening.

The opening did not seem to go too deep under the hill; but there was no way of being sure how far in it led; or whether, if he should try to swim into it, he might not find himself trapped underwater with no way to turn about and with drowning inevitable. He thought longingly of the underwater breathing equipment he could have had included in with his other hidden tools, if it had only occurred to him that he would be faced with a situation like this one.

Then inspiration came to him. He crowded his body into the opening, blocking out light from the open underwater behind him, and turned off the torch. It took a few seconds for his eyes to adjust and he was just starting to feel that he must get back to breath and air, when he began to distinguish a dim, but unmistakable illumination ahead of him through the water.

With bursting lungs, he backed out of the opening, and rose to the surface to breathe.

After a moment, with a once more reoxygenated body, he dived again. This time he kept the torch off on his way down; and when he looked into the hole, he was able to adjust his eyes quickly enough to see that its further end was only about five meters further on and emerged into water with light glancing through it. He went back up, filled his lungs once more, dove down and swam boldly through the natural tunnel.

He broke surface a second later in the still waters of a high-ceilinged grotto, into which light soared in thin rays from what seemed to be a number of tiny openings about its walls. As his vision adjusted further to this dim illumination, he saw a sort of ledge across some fifteen meters of water to his right, a ledge flanked by two unlit wall-torches and a flight of steps cut in the stone, leading up to some more strongly lit region above.

Harb trod water for a second while he filled his lungs, then turned and dived again, out the tunnel and back up on to the bank outside.

He went in search of Rajn, feeling a certain smugness. The smugness lasted until he came in sight of the cooking fire against which the bulk of the Homskarter King was recognizable. Then, for the first time, it occurred to Harb to wonder if the Homskarters could swim — or if perhaps they had some deep-grained taboo or fear of putting their heads under water. All at once the easy road to conquest of the high city which he had discovered did not look all that easy. But it was too late to go

back and think the situation over again. Rajn had already caught sight of him.

"Outlander! Here!" Rajn was calling.

The king looked in a grim mood. As Harb came up, he found himself uncomfortably aware of the other's dark eyes, deep-set under the heavy brow-ridge and holding steadily fixed on Harb.

"Well?" said Rajn, as Harb stepped before him. "What have you to tell me?"

Harb gambled against the risk of triggering a temper reaction in the King before being given a chance to explain.

"Nothing, King," he said deliberately.

"Nothing?" Rajn's voice deepened. About the two of them the other Homskarters were silent and motionless, watching.

"Nothing to tell you, King," said Harb easily, "but something to show you. Will you come with me?"

For a moment Rajn did not move or answer. Then he stepped forward.

"Show me what you have to show," he said. The nearby Homskarters moved forward also, but Rajn looked at them and they checked.

"We will go alone," he said. "Lead on, Outlander."

Harb conducted him to the spot on the bank above the entrance to the grotto; and began to strip off his clothes.

"There's a way into the mountain, King," he said. "If you'll come with me down under the water I can show it to you."

He was watching Rajn closely as he said this. If the King was no swimmer, or had any large fear of the water, now was the moment for Harb to discover it. But Rajn showed no hesitation whatever. He unstrapped his body armor and dropped it on the ground. He undid his sheathed sword from his belt and laid it with the armor. However, the belt itself, together with the long knife in its sheath that was still attached to the belt, he kept on.

"Just below the bank here, King," said Harb, "underwater, there is a hole into which we can swim that leads into a cave half-filled with water, inside the mountain. There are steps leading down into the cave from above and I believe that they lead up to the city. If you'll follow me, I'll show this cave to you."

He went down into the water and ducked under the surface without waiting for the Homskarter to answer. A second after there was a heavy splash and Rajn joined him. Crouched against the sloping underwater bank, Harb pointed to the entrance to the grotto. Without hesitation Rajn pushed past him and pulled himself into the dark opening.

Harb felt a brief twinge of reluctant admiration, remembering how he himself had hesitated to enter that unknown aperture when he had first discovered it. But Rajn's hair-dark legs were already disappearing into the opening. Harb followed him.

They both broke surface inside the grotto — with some noise in that echoing interior, but happily there was no one from the city above waiting there who might have heard them. Harb pointed to the ledge with the unlit torches. They swam to it and pulled themselves out on its cold and slippery surface, which gleamed, like the stone walls about them, with condensed moisture.

Rajn, however, paid no attention to the ledge or the torches but went directly to the steps and climbed up them for a short distance, peering into the gloom higher up. Unlike the grotto, dimly lit with light leaking in through what must be small apertures in the hillside, the steps evidently ascended through the solid interior limestone of the hill and a little way up them the darkness was complete. Rajn came back down the steps.

"Come," he said.

They reentered the water and swam back out to the light and air of the outside world.

"We'll need torches," the Homskarter king said as he rebuckled his body armor about him. "Stay close beside me, Outlander. There's much to do."

The afternoon was already moving into its later stages. Rajn explained matters briefly to Witta and some of the other chieftains and put them on the alert to gather fighters and storm the city gates if they should see evidence of these being opened from within, or fire within the city. Then he gathered an expeditionary force of some twenty of his own Homskarters, weeding out those few who were not, like himself, good swimmers, and gathered a bundle of the large torches that had been part of their loot from the last conquest. These were a porous wood which had been steeped in vats of vegetable oil. They stank unbelievably, as Harb already knew from experience, but they would be able to stand a brief immersion and — once dried off again — still light.

With this crew and Harb, who was beginning to worry and had cast about in his mind for some excuse to keep himself apart from what seemed to be the primary assault force, they returned to the inside of the grotto. But to Harb's surprise, Rajn did not immediately light his torches and lead his warriors up the steps. To those among his own people who questioned him on that same point, he answered with succinct generalship.

"We'll wait for some to come down from the city," he said. "Then slay them and go up. If we can kill quietly enough, those above will only think we are their own people returning."

So they waited — in the clammy darkness. It seemed an unbearable as well as an interminable wait, but eventually voices were heard down the stairwell, though these were distorted by echoes to unintelligibility, and finally a light was seen from above, growing stronger as whoever carrying it descended.

Rajn gestured them all off the ledge into the water.

Footsteps and grumbling accompanied the growing illumination, and finally a native with the rounder face and tufted ears of the plains dwellers reached the ledge, blinking around with his eyes dazzled by his torch against the grotto's dimness. With one hand he balanced a huge stack of what looked like empty wine-skins on his shoulder. He used the torch to light the nearer of the two torches on the stone wall above the ledge, put his own light out and dropped his skins. He shouted up into the darkness where sight of the grotto walls were swallowed up, overhead.

There was a momentary wait and then, unexpectedly, the end of a rope fell from that same darkness to the ledge.

Still grumbling to himself about something, the native attached the rope to one of his empty skins, dropped it in the water off the edge of the ledge and dragged it back and forth until it swelled with liquid. Then he shouted upwards again and the line went taut. To a creaking sound from above the now full waterskin was hauled up into invisibility.

Chilled in the water, watching, Harb could not believe his eyes. The waterskin, full, must have been nearly as heavy as the native himself. Nothing Harb had seen on this world implied rope manufacture and other technologies that could conveniently lift such a weight through a couple of hundred of vertical feet of ascension.

But he had no time for further consideration of that point, because Rajn himself had already silently emerged from the water behind the city native, with several of the other warriors behind him. They reached the waterskin handler in a silent rush. There was a brief explosion of action, and the city native dropped with only a half-strangled cry that was almost more of a grunt. Gratefully Harb climbed out of the chilling water with the others, once more onto the ledge.

Leaving one warrior to tend the dropped rope with additional filled waterskins, so that those above would not be alerted to any difference from below, Rajn led the expedition up the stairs. They had not climbed more than fifty feet when they reached a small room cut into the rock, and Harb saw the explanation of how the windskins were lifted. Here, at this much more practical distance for such primitives, was a windlass manned by

two of the city natives. The line from it was taut and descended to the water below. Behind them was another rope, descending, obviously, from another such room fifty feet higher again, so that the waterskins could be lifted in stages.

Once more, there was the sudden rush, the minimum of noise in killing, and the expedition climbed again. At the next windlass room, the scene was repeated, and so they continued upward, taking over the waterlift system as they went, until they emerged finally into a room containing a full dozen of the city natives.

Not all of these were armed and ready. But silence was impossible. The stone-walled chamber they inhabited rang and thundered for a few minutes until all the city natives, and three of the invaders, lay still on the floor. Harb looked around. They had plainly reached the top of the conveyor system. A large supply of the waterskins, empty, were stacked in the back of the room, and to their left was a barred door to which Rajn was already headed.

Harb went to join the Homskarter king. Rajn lifted the bar and opened the door slightly. He grunted under his breath in humorous self-congratulation.

"Look for yourself, Outlander," he said to Harb. "We have them."

Harb looked. Plainly the place they were in was half-cave half-constructed room. It was in one of the stone buildings that seemed to nestle against the hill at a point where the rise of the hillside was somewhat steeper than normal. Below them were the roofs of a line of mud-brick buildings and be-

yond them, the city gates — closed, but guarded by what looked like no more than a half-dozen sentries. The attention of all these sentries was directed outward over the walls.

"Go back the way we came, Outlander," Rajn said. "Tell Witta we'll open that gate for him as soon as it's full dark. He should be close by, with warriors enough to hold it while the rest of the expedition follows."

Harb went, feeling a great relief at having been offered this easy way of dodging the area of actual fighting.

At the foot of the hill, when Harb found him, Witta glared at Harb suspiciously all the time Harb was giving his message; but when Harb was done the Homskarter second-in-command swung about to the other chieftains and petty kings who had been gathered to listen.

"You heard the words of King Rajn from this outlander!" said Witta. "Tell your men. As soon as twilight deepens all should begin to move up to the wall . . . quietly."

His eyes swung and focused on Harb.

"And you, Outlander," he said. "I want you by my side."

Harb's only choice was to accept. So it developed that in the taking of the high city that followed he went with Witta to the very foot of the city wall before there was a sudden gout of flame and smoke inside it, a hundred yards or so away from the gates, and the roar of excited voices.

"Now!" growled Witta. And, as if on cue, the gates creaked and opened. In the rush that started for them, as the forest natives at last forgot everything but the fighting and Harb was finally able to fall behind, to fade back through the other roaring invaders coming up behind Witta's party and so reach the beach again with a whole skin.

He was careful to stay there until the invaders started straggling back down, laden with booty. Above them on the hillside the high city burned merrily with a dozen separate fires. Before the first of the warriors could recognize him and re-member finding him with the boats on their re-turn, Harb had slipped away from the camp and he did not come in again until most of those who had gone up the hill in the twilight were back down it again.

When he did return to camp, he detoured by the canots before circling to make his appearance seem as if he was just now coming back down the hillside. To his satisfaction the craft were finally loaded with plunder. Their cargo areas were full. The high city had been an even richer plum than Harb himself had expected.

"Congratulations, king!" he said, when he at last found a — probably only seemingly — drunken Rajn by the royal Homskarter cooking fire. "Your canots lie deep in the water. No more room for loot, now!"

Rajn coughed with uproarious laughter.

"Always more room for loot, Outlander!" he said. "Always more room. We merely throw out the less good to make more room for the better!"

For a moment Harb thought that the other was joking, that what he was saying was only another example of the rather cruel native humor that got its greatest pleasure out of confounding and frustrating its target. Then his hopes plummeted as he understood something he should have realized before.

It was not for loot alone that the forest natives took the summer trail to the plains. It was for excitement — for entertainment. Why should they turn back now, when there were still cities to take and plains people to kill?

He had been an idiot. Of course, the expedition would not turn back until casualties had reached the point where the survivors began to worry seriously about their ability to fight their way safely home with what they had won. The summer was advancing and Harb with his aid to them had been making it possible for them to stay longer in the plains, not pushing them toward the day when they would turn back early with slaves and grain.

But maybe he could still talk sense to Rajn.

"A wise king keeps what he gets," Harb said. "Would it not be wise to turn back now?"

"Oh, wise indeed, Outlander!" said Rajn thickly. "Wise indeed."

Harb felt a sudden, leaping relief.

"Then we go back?" he asked.

"How can you think such a thing of me, Outlander?" hiccuped Rajn, "after you've pleaded with me so strongly otherwise? Of course we go on — to take those rich islands in a lake you've been so eager for us to loot!"

When they reached the lake five days later, it was after a long paddle upstream against the current; and at the end of the trip were the falls by which the lake spilled out to form the river, so that the canots had all to be unloaded and portaged up around the falls, a labor that put most of the warriors in a bad temper.

However, at the top of the falls, a little way around the lake they took over a cluster of lakeside fishing villages which, though they were too poor to have any loot worthy of the name and their frail lake-going craft excited nothing but contempt on the part of the forest natives, were still a ready supply of shelter, food and servants. Also, the weather was now delightful, and the expedition, having treated itself to a three-day drunk to celebrate the hard work of getting here, began to be in better humor.

One of the first things Rajn did was bring in one of the fishing village natives for questioning about the islands and their inhabitants. There had been a certain amount of concern among the members of the expedition when they reached the lake and saw nothing but a watery horizon as far as their eyes could sweep. They had indeed heard the warning relayed from Harb that the islands would be out of sight from the shore that surrounded the lake, but they had preferred not to believe it. Nothing in their experience had made it possible to envision a body of water that big. It was much easier simply to assume that outlanders had weak eyes.

It was with some relief, then, that a good many of the chieftains and petty kings heard the villager corroborate the fact that the islands and their people existed.

"What are they like, then, you?" demanded one of the kings.

The fishing villager rolled his gaze to the one

who had spoken. He was plainly hoping against hope that he would not be killed as part of the questioning process; but there was also a sort of fatalism about him that seemed to lead him to give less careful and politic answers than a human might have in a like situation.

"Like you," he said.

"Like us? How — like us?" growled Witta.

"Thieves with swords. Takers. Just like you."

"Indeed," said Rajn, coughing a laugh, "they sound like interesting opponents. How far from here are their islands?"

The villager looked at him and blinked, without answering. Obviously he could find no way of expressing the answer Rajn had demanded. After a moment, he made a try at answering.

"In half a day with one of our boats," he said at last. "You can see them. In early evening you come to them. But your boats haven't any sails."

He was referring to the simple lugsail with which each of the village fishing craft were equipped.

"We can have sails if we wish," Witta retorted. It was true, Harb remembered from his studies. When the wind was from the right direction, the forest canots would sometimes hoist a scrap of square sail in their bows to assist them on trips over the long, winding stretches where they occasionally travelled for kilometers without putting into shore.

"Indeed," said Rajn, again, "and I think we could well use them on so long a trip. We must rig some. If these cockle-shells they use here make the trip in one long day, we should certainly be able to do the same in no more than a little more time and

probably in less. Let this one and some others — "
he pointed to the villager, "be put to work doing
that."

And the villager was hustled off to that purpose,
quite cheerful still to be alive.

However, as early as the following morning,
difficulties appeared. The villagers, in their own
way, were as conservative as any of the other natives. There was very little difference between the
rigging of a square bowsail and the rigging of a
lugsail. But it was too much of a difference for a
people who believed that anything that was not a
lugsail was not a sail at all. The forest natives took
over the rigging of their sails, making a game of it,
splashing and swimming around the shallow
water of the shore to the amazement of the apparently non-swimming villagers, who were
horrified to see them in the water.

The expedition warriors gibed at the timidity of
the villagers; and a high time was had by all the
invaders until one of their number, swimming by
himself, started to scream and thrash in the water — and a moment later disappeared, leaving
only a bloody stain that rose to the surface and
started to spread.

Before the rest could get out of the water, either
into dry land or into one of the moored canots,
four others had been attacked and pulled under.

"Killers!" shouted the villagers excitedly. "Killers!"

"What killers?" roared Rajn in a towering rage.
He picked up one of the villagers and raised him in
both arms to throw him into the water. "What killers"

The villager screamed with terror.

"Look! Look!" he cried.

Rajn looked and dropped the other, absently. Luckily for him, the villager fell at the edge of the dock on which they were standing and was able to keep himself from going into the lake. Rajn strode out to the end of the dock and peered down into the meter-deep water at which the villager had been pointing.

Harb followed after him and saw that the water held a fast-moving swarm of fish, all about the same length — about that of his forearm. They had stubby bodies and were big-bodied just behind the head, but the head itself and the jaws beyond it were like those of a barracuda. Harb looked at Rajn, expecting a further explosion of fury; but the Homskarter king now looked more interested than angry.

"So that's why these hairless-eared fisherfolk can't swim," he said. He turned to the villager he had almost dropped into the lake. "Come here!"

The villager came, fearfully.

"Where do they come from?" Rajn demanded, pointing at the fish. It was the question Harb himself had wanted to ask.

"They live in the weeds of the shallow water near the shore. When they think there's food near, they come out. They kill anything they can reach."

"So," said Rajn. "Do they also live in weeds around the islands we're going to?"

"Anywhere there are weeds," said the villager.

"So. We're wiser now, then," said Rajn, looking thoughtfully back into the water where the fish still darted about, "than we were a few minutes ago. The rest of the sail-rigging will have to be

done with the canots moored to the docks."

This new restriction slowed down work on the sails. Nonetheless, two days later, they were all ready to set out. The weather had been hot for a week, and once they were well out from shore they got a breeze that their sails could use. Happily, the warriors stripped off their arm-paddles and relaxed to enjoy the ride.

Pleasant, it undeniably was. Speedy, it was not. It became obvious to Harb early in the day that their speed was probably not much more than three-quarters of that possible to the lighter fisher craft with their lugsails, and without the plunder that weighed down the already heavy canots. When evening came there were still no islands in sight; although they could still see the shore they had left, as a faint line on the horizon far behind them.

They tied the canots together for the night and took down the sails until daybreak. The leaders in the various canots kept a strict control over the evening drinking, so there was little in the way of incident. Still, Harb prudently changed places two times to put some distance between himself and altercations that broke out; and he ended up perched on the very bow of the canot, hidden from the others by the pile of furs and personal belongings that occupied the forepart of the boat's forecastle — Rajn's territory.

He had found himself a fairly comfortable niche, burrowed into the back of this pile, and was dozing off — when he felt a sudden shove and saw the water coming up toward him as he went overboard. He had a glimpse of a Homskarter face he thought might be Witta's, staring down at him with a curious expression in which both terror

and triumph seemed to be mixed — then the water closed over him and he came snorting to the surface, swimming furiously to make up for the fact he was trying to bear up under the weight of his sword and armor. These things, though designed to be as light as possible, were heavy enough to drown him if he could not get to safety quickly, and he was grateful for the hairy hands that caught him a moment later, and drew him back on board before he was exhausted.

He stood in the cargo area, dripping, the whole boat alive with coughing laughter as the Homskarters there laughed at him.

"The outlander wanted a drink!" shouted someone. "Why didn't you ask me, Outlander? I had a little ale left!"

"Why didn't the killers get him?" somebody asked, and the humor died in a new seriousness.

"Because there aren't any out here. They live around the shore weeds, not in deep water!" snarled Harb, too furious to think. He was looking around the faces surrounding him for Witta, but the Homskarter second-in-command unaccountably was not to be seen.

Abruptly, Harb remembered to take advantage of this change to turn their reaction to his advantage.

"In any case," he added, "we outlanders have ways many don't know. We aren't easy to kill" — once more he looked around for Witta, but could not make him out — "and those who try it always live to regret it. Many fish and even animals know this and often they'll avoid attacking us."

"A magic life, Outlander?" said the voice of Rajn, with irony; and Harb knew that the king, at least, had not been convinced by his implication of strange powers in humans. On the other hand, if it had indeed been Witta who had pushed him overboard, hoping that the predator fish would take care of him, Harb was fairly certain Rajn had not been involved in the attempt. At least, not as long as Harb was still useful to the Homskarter king.

Dawn came finally. They hoisted their sails, caught the breeze once more and by morning caught sight of something on the water far ahead that finally resolved itself in land of some sort. They were well out of sight of the shore now; and evidently they had drifted off their line of sailing during the night, for what they saw were at an angle to the way they were headed.

They corrected course and the land began to get larger, revealing itself at last as what certainly looked like an island, lying low and green in the sea.

Perversely, hardly had they sighted it than the wind changed direction, pushing them away from it. However, the sight of land had raised the warriors spirits. With a good deal of noise and a certain amount of horseplay, the sails were hauled down; and the paddlers went energetically to work.

At first they could hardly tell they were making progress. But gradually the island seemed to lengthen in front of them and lift itself higher above the waves. After that, changes began to be visible in more rapid sequence. The island grew steadily in size and a low rise of hills covered by vegetation became discernable, above the whiter strip of shore. This change continued until it became plain that they were headed toward a bay, beyond which some of the sharper-eyed could swear that they saw structures of some sort. Estimates began to be made as to how soon they would actually touch shore again, with some of the optimistic placing that moment at the native equivalent of less than an hour off, when something new was seen.

Without warning, appearing as if by magic from nowhere — it took Harb a moment to realise they were emerging from behind a headland of the bay — were three moving shapes. Even at this distance it was possible to make out that they were boats; and as he watched they turned to head directly toward the fleet of canots and came on.

Aboard the canots the warriors had fallen silent. For now that they had the distance to the land to use as a yard-stick, these three craft coming to meet them obviously could be seen to be large, indeed. The canots were several times the size of the village craft they had seen back on the lake shore. But these three vessels coming were each double or more the length of the largest canot and high-sided, as well as decked, in proportion. They rode steadily on the small waves which managed to rock the canots, they each had one large square sail forward, and they were propelled in addition not by arm paddles — their sides were far too high for that — but by long oars for which their sides were pierced.

At the bow each one had a high painted prow with a beak built into it at the water line and an open forecastle upon which a number of figures began to be visible as the two fleets drew together at the sum of their combined speeds through the water. As the three island craft came closer, a steady sound began to carry over the water to the canots. It was the regular clanging of something that sounded like an off-key cymbal, or perhaps just a strip of ordinary iron being hammered steadily and rhythmically by just another such strip of iron. And, as the three island vessels came close enough for real details to be seen, the warriors in the canots could make out that the figures on each of the elevated forecastles and sterncastles wore some kind of high, plumed headdress and stood beside a mechanism of some sort.

At first the warriors in the canots had been struck into an awe-filled silence by the sheer size of the boats coming toward them. Now, however, that these craft were closer, a reaction began to set in. At first scattered, and then general, yells and waving of weapons began to erupt among the canots, and the paddlers bent to their work. The forest dwellers began to take heart from the number of their canots compared to the craft opposing them — who were three only, even if large; and a wave of enthusiasm for the coming conflict seemed to race through the canots like a forest fire through treetops.

The canots swarmed toward the three island vessels. The three came on steadily, in V-formation, one leading, the other two flanking and trailing. Suddenly, it seemed, they and the canots were only a few canot-lengths apart. Then, with no lapse of time at all, they had come together.

The leading two canots made the mistake of meeting the first island ship head on. Her beak tossed the first one aside, splitting it open as it did so; and the second one was literally ridden under the surface of the water, as the island vessel rammed and sank her.

Abruptly, the three were surrounded by the canots; and for the first time the mechanisms on each raised forecastle went into action. These proved to be a form of shaft-firing ballistae, each one like a monster crossbow shooting a quarrel as large as an ordinary spear. Where one of these struck a canot, they pierced two or three warriors at once or went clear through the bottom of it. At the same time, other figures had raised up all along the sides of the island vessels and were hurling large rocks down into the surrounding canots; and these rocks also felled warriors, or tore through the bottoms of the smaller vessels.

But the most devastating effect was that through all this action the oarsmen of the island craft, protected by the high, sturdy sides of their vessel, continued to row. On the canots all paddling had automatically ceased with the moment of meeting the enemy. But under the steady drive of their oars the island vessels drew clear, turned, and came back at their own equivalent of flank speed.

They crashed into a fleet of canots that this time were a picture of confusion. Some canots were trying to close with the opposing boats, some were desperately trying to avoid being beaked or ridden under. In this confusion the island craft had a holiday. They cut another murderous swath through the fleet of canots and turned to come back a third time.

But by now, however, the pickings had suddenly

become much leaner. The canots had learned their lesson, which was to disperse. They might not be able to match the island vessels in straight-away speed, but with their paddlers in action they were much more agile. The few that the island craft came close to, dodged out of the way of the larger vessels with no difficulty. Gradually the canots drew off and lay in a ring around the larger boats and the large boats ceased rowing.

It was, plainly, a standoff. If the warriors in the canots could have boarded the three other boats, their overwhelming numbers would have given them victory in short order. But they could not board without getting close, and they could not get close without being rammed or sunk by missiles. On the other hand, if the canots had only remained still in close formation, the islanders could have run through and sunk them all in short orders; but the canots were no longer being obliging in that respect.

On his own, much lower forecastle, Rajn snarled under his breath, staring at the three enemy craft.

"Outlander!" he shouted. "Outlander, come here!"

Back in the central part of the canot, Harb rose reluctantly and went forward. No hands were extended to shove him — the native caution where unknown powers of the outlanders was still in existence to a certain extent — but he could feel the savage fury and animosity of the figures around him as if it was a heat emanating from their hairy bodies. He came up, mounted the forecastle and stood beside Rajn.

"Yes, king?" he said.

"Outlander!" snapped Rajn. "Look around. This

was your idea — to come here. Five cities haven't cost us as much in men as we've just lost to foes who have not even had one of their own people bruised by us! You got us here. You tell us how to conquer those craft!"

Harb took a deep breath. His mind had been racing ever since the moment of the first disastrous closing with the island vessels. He had only one answer in mind; and if it did not work, there would be no escape for him, trapped on a small boat in the center of a lake like this.

"Had you asked me before your canots charged at these ships, king," he said boldly, "I could have saved you a great many of the warriors you have lost. But I was not asked. Now, it's true, you've lost a good deal of your strength; but there is still a way to victory if the warriors will do exactly what I say."

Rajn stared at him. That stare was not easy to meet; but Harb met it.

"Say on," said Rajn, with ominous quietness.

"The canots cannot get close to the island boats without being run down and sunk," said Harb. "But there is another way to get warriors aboard these craft to take them."

Harb pointed at a last few of the forest natives from the sunken canots who had not yet been picked up. One of the island craft backed water on its left oars and swung suddenly toward three of these. It seemed to be right on top of them, but at the last moment all three disappeared — only to reappear a moment later out of reach on the far side of the boat.

"Swim to them," Harb said, "go underwater when close, then surface all around the ship at once and climb aboard—up the oars or any other

127

way there is. It won't be easy but it can be done."

He stopped speaking. Rajn still looked at him. From behind Harb, Witta's voice said one word.

"Killers."

"Are killers attacking those men in the water out there?" said Harb without turning around. "Did killers attack me, when somehow"— he emphasized the word slightly—"I went overboard last night? As I told you all then, the killers are only in the shore water, not out here."

He stopped again. Still, there was silence. Silently, fervently and internally he hoped that there were not other, large fish operating as predators in these deeper waters. It was plain that finally he had come to a time when he could not get by on words alone. He took off his sword belt, threw off his body armor and rebelted the sword about his waist.

"Follow me," he said, and dove over the side.

He dared not look back to see if any were following him until he was well underway toward the nearest island ship. Then, it turned out to be unnecessary, as he began to be passed up by swimming Homskarters. Soon, the water around him was full of bodies.

The island craft saw them coming and turned toward them. Stones and the large spears began to fly. Harb dived, swam a short distance underwater just to hide his whereabouts from anyone on the island ship who might have picked him as a specific target, and then resurfaced . . . and panicked.

He had misjudged the speed with which the island ship could approach them. The vessel was almost on top of him.

Stiff with fear, he dove deep, and heard the beat of oars and saw the shadow of the island boat's keel passing above him. All about him in the underwater were other forest natives. They came up together, gasping for air behind the island craft, which had now halted. Warriors about Harb were climbing oars, swarming up the sides of the boat.

A madness came over Harb. He forgot entirely that being without his shield he was effectively without the whole bag of tricks he counted on to keep himself safe. He found himself clambering up over the side of the boat. A native within swung an axe at him, but he tumbled inside the boat and the axe flashed over his head, burying itself in the boat's side. As its owner tried to wrench it free, Harb drew his sword, reached up and drove it through the other's body. Then he was fighting an individual in a plumed headdress and the action dissolved into a blur . . .

Harb came back to himself gradually. He was lying on something soft that moved rhythmically and he felt queasy. Both his head and his neck ached. Slowly he came fully awake and realized he was lying on the cargo in the mid-section of Rajn's ship. It was early morning and they were travelling.

He tried to sit up, but at the first movement a sharp pain seemed to enter his right temple just above his eye and probe back and down into his neck and left shoulder. He gritted his teeth however and did sit up. Gingerly he put his hand up to his head and found it crusty and rough with dried blood that had turned his hair into an asphalt-like lump and poured down evidently as far as the base of his skull.

"Awake, Outlander?" said the voice of Rajn. "It's time."

Harb tried to speak; but all that came out of his mouth was a croak. He moved stiffly, his head stabbing him at each movement until he could get to the open ale barrel standing broached just beyond the cargo section. He drank from its unpleasant-tasting contents without caring that he had no lemon-flavored pill to disguise them. All that mattered was the chance to swallow water or the next available thing to it.

With the liquid in him, he felt a little better. Reviving, he was conscious of a black and burning hatred toward Rajn for making it necessary for him to get himself injured in this way. But he dared not show those feelings to the Homskarter king. He swallowed and spoke.

"What happened to me?"

"I don't think it was an axe or a sword, Outlander," said Rajn, coughing humorously. "Either one would have split your skull open, instead of just denting it a little. Maybe it was a mixing spoon, or a baby's toy."

"Where are we?"

"Headed home, of course," said Rajn. His jocularity faded. "There are other islands and other ships, it seems. We'll come back ready to take them all next year. Meanwhile, there were some good pickings in that one bay. We'll even bring back your grain and prisoners — only we'll pick them up closer to home on the way back."

Harb looked at him, marvelling.

"How long have I . . ."

"Slumbered? Two days now," said Rajn.

"Two days!" Harb felt a stab of anxiety. He must have had a concussion. A concussion could be deadly out here beyond modern medical aid. On the other hand, he had already survived two days; so possibly he was all right.

So they started back to the forest villages, though not without some difficulties. There still remained those who wished to continue the sword-trail simply for the pleasure of killing and looting, even though they would not be able to carry home any more than they had now. This attitude, however, was met by strong objections from Rajn and the lesser chiefs, who clearly saw their individual advantage of taking home as many healthy warriors as possible. Finally, there was the religious question involved in carrying back such a large number of slaves as Harb wanted, slaves who would be only potential sacrifices. Might not the Gods be annoyed by being made to wait for these sacrifices?

The argument for this went on for a number of days before it dawned on Harb that no one was serious about it. The forest warriors were merely soothing their consciences by finding excuses to do what they intended to do in any case.

At last, all discussion over, they loaded their canots and headed upstream. By this time Harb

had completely recovered from his head injury.
This was slower going than the downstream trip;
but they were aided by a light, if prevailing wind
from the south at this time of year. Each canot
hoisted a rag of a sail — much more than a rag,
Harb judged, and a canot would run a real risk of
overturning in a gust — and with this to aid them,
found themselves back in the shadows of the
forest vegetation within three weeks.

From this point on, the return went swiftly,
since most of their travel was across lakes where
there was no current against them. There was a
parting celebration at each community where any
sizeable number of warriors dropped off, and a
friendly wrangle over how many of the slaves
should be taken by those who were parting from
the main body. This was a drain on the number of

captured villagers that Harb had not foreseen. He
could not complain about it openly, but he ground
his teeth in private. It shortened his already
strained temper, under pressure with the need of
keeping up the appearance of enjoying the return.

The truth of the matter was that in spite of his
self-training before coming to 49381D, he was not
really emotionally acclimated to living in canot-
close proximity to the natives of this world for
some days on end. Sharing a narrow fifty-foot boat
with them was a little like occupying the same
amount of space with a shoulder-to-shoulder pack
of wild animals with the gift of speech and the skill
to use weapons. They were essentially as dangerous as predatory animals, as unwashed, as reac-
tive, and as unpredictable in their emotional reactions. When they were not working, sleeping, or

eating, they were either quarreling or playing the most primitive of practical jokes on each other.

Harb found himself taking any excuse at all to get away by himself. So it happened that on one of the occasions when a fair-sized group was parting from the expeditions and the usual party was in progress, that Harb wandered off into the woods for an hour or two of privacy. Luckily, as he stepped into the concealment of the branches, he

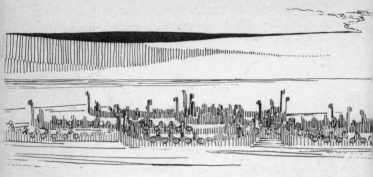

switched the heat sensor unit in his helmet into
connection with an alarm beamed to his inner ear;
because some fifteen minutes later the alarm went
off.

Automatically, Harb flipped down the heat-sensing visor and turned on his heel, searching the
thick undergrowth for the aura that had triggered
the alarm. He found it behind him, upwind. There
was nothing in sight to ordinary vision, but the
scale at the side of the screen was reading a body
the size of a male warrior, some twenty feet away
through the thick vegetation. Harb thought
quickly, and took a chance with a guess.

"Witta!" he shouted cheerfully, crashing
through the brush loudly and openly toward the
Homskarter. "What brings you out here?"

With the last words he broke through a final
screen of small branches and saw Witta standing,
scowling at him. The vice-king was wearing his

sword but no shield, which might catch on branches and make noise going through thick woods. Instead, he had a bow and quiver of arrows slung on his back and carried a spear.

"Hunting," grunted Witta. But the vice-king was a poor liar. His self-consciousness of the falsehood he had just uttered showed in every line of his body, like the guilty crouch of a dog who has been sleeping on a forbidden sofa until the moment before its owners came home.

"Good idea," said Harb, cheerfully. "I'll hunt with you. Side by side."

"I'm through hunting," muttered Witta. He turned and crashed away in the direction of the others. Harb followed him.

After that, Harb took to setting the alarm of the heat sensor at no less than fifty feet of range whenever he went into the woods alone. But Witta did not try to sneak up on him again. The fact that Harb had been able to not only discover the vice-king but identify him, and this when Witta was unseen with the wind blowing from Harb to him, apparently had awed the vice-king.

The farewell parties along the way slowed them down and took their toll of the available slaves; but in time they did return to the lands of the Homskarters. The night before they were due to arrive at the Homskarter village, Harb drew Rajn aside.

"What is it now, Outlander?" Rajn asked, eyeing Harb shrewdly as they walked along the lake shore out of hearing of the rest of the Homskarters.

"About the slaves," Harb said.

"Ho, now it comes out at last," said Rajn,

humorously. "Tell me. What about the slaves, Out-lander?"

"It's still only late spring here, King," he said "There'd still be time to get one crop in the ground and harvested before fall; and you have seed-grain to spare from the grain which you brought from the plains."

"I told you we were no farmers."

"True," said Harb. "But the slaves are farm-ers — not only farmers, but experienced farmers, who have grown up in the craft of bringing food from the soil."

"The slaves," said Rajn, "will be sacrificed as promised as soon as we are home."

"I know that was promised," said Harb. He had a feeling of walking on eggs. How much did Rajn really believe in his Gods? There was no way of telling. "But what great harm could there be in putting off the sacrifice until after a harvest has been gotten in?

"The Gods might weary of waiting and turn their anger against us," said Rajn. But he said it without particular emotion, as a more industrialized man might mention the prospect of an economic turndown. "Besides, we have enough grain to see us through the winter. Enough and more."

"But there may be other forest villages and homesteads who may run short," said Harb. "In which case, if you had grain to spare, you could trade it to them when their bellies begin to pinch, and glean for yourself the best of their wealth . . ." he paused, to give time for the idea to sink in. "Perhaps, for the food they need to live until spring. Then when next you go on the sword-trail, you would be so strong that the lesser chiefs would not even dare to argue with you."

Rajn said nothing. They continued walking along the shore together in silence. Eventually, Harb broke it.

"This is the way a king may become greater," he said.

Rajn stopped and turned to face Harb, who had no choice but to stop also and face the native.

"Outlander," said Rajn, "I'm not sure but what you want is to push us into ways unfitting for warriors. Still . . . if I wished to use these slaves to plant grain, as you say, what could I say to my people? Few among them will come easily to the idea of putting off the Gods a second time."

"Tell them you'll give the Gods a token sacrifice — kill a single slave as earnest of the sacrifice of all in the fall."

Rajn stood a moment, then turned and began walking back toward the camp. Harb fell in beside him.

"I will give you this much, Outlander. You may suggest this action to me, tonight when we sit around the fire," Rajn said after a moment. "Let it come from you and I will listen to what my men answer."

"All right," said Harb. They walked on a few steps more. "By the way, could I also have two of the slaves for myself? A man and a woman, preferably two who're fond of each other?"

Rajn looked at him.

"Such a gift is small return for what you have done for us," the king said. "Choose your pair and be welcome."

144

"Thanks," said Harb.

That afternoon, Harb picked out his slaves. In actuality, he had had his eye on the pair he wanted for some time. He collected them from the separate camp where the slaves were bedded down and told them to come with him and stay with him. The plains people did not speak a mutually understandable tongue with the forest warriors, but the slaves had already learned some of the forest language and signs conveyed the rest of Harb's message. Actually, Harb had trained himself as well in the plains' tongue as in Rajn's, but it would hardly have been wise to let the Homskarters hear him talking plains speech fluently with two of their captives.

That night at the king's fire in the warrior's camp, once Rajn, Witta and the rest of the Homskarters close to the king had reached what Harb judged to be the optimum stage of alcoholic mellowness, Harb got to his feet.

"King," he said, "I have had an idea which you might wish to consider."

"Tell us, Outlander," answered Rajn, blurring his words only slightly. He glanced at the Homskarter faces around the fire producing an immediate silence, and added pleasantly. "Your ideas are always welcome. Some, like the thought that we might take that city we conquered just before coming home, have proved quite worthy."

"Thank you, king," said Harb. He glanced over his shoulder to make sure his two new slaves were standing side by side at his back as he had ordered them to, once he stood up. He looked back at Rajn and the warriors. "It came to my mind that this winter when food gets scarce for those of other villages who have not won as much in prizes on the sword-trail, that you and your Homskarters might gain both wealth and power by trading grain to those less fortunate, for whatever price might be obtained."

There was a moment's pause, then a slow mutter of approval generally around the fire. Only Witta and several warriors sitting on either side of him sat grimly with closed mouths.

"A thought worth telling," said Rajn nodding. "Not but that I should have thought of it myself probably, when the snow was deep. But there is no knowing whether we will have much extra grain to trade. We must make sure our own bellies don't go empty first."

"King," said Harb, "there is a way you might have all the grain your bellies need and yet have ample to trade with."

"And how is that, Outlander?"

Harb pointed toward the slave camp.

"You now have slaves who are skilled at raising grain," he said. "Put them to labor in fields through the summer and store up riches of food to be used as you wish."

"Those slaves are promised to the Gods!" snapped Witta. "By summer their bodies will be nothing but dry bones!"

"Could not the Gods wait until fall? I am an Outlander, and of course don't know the answer to questions like this," added Harb, hastily, as the ring of faces and bodies about the fire went rigidly still, "but it occurs to me to ask if the Gods wouldn't be willing to wait, just this once."

146

"They've waited already!" said Witta. He swung on Rajn. "Cousin and king, are we to flout Gods? Gods who can send us a winter that never ends? Gods who can turn our blades aside from the foe when we next go on the sword-trail?"

"Forgive me!" Harb raised his voice above Witta's. "I meant no disrespect to the Gods. But if they are truly the Gods of the Homskarters, I'd think for their own benefit they'd wish to see the Homskarters grow strong and bring them back many slaves for sacrifice every year — not just one. And it isn't as if they're being cheated of their present sacrifice. We need only to send them a messenger promising them that after the harvest is in all slaves will be sent to them, as well as many slaves each year from now on, when the Homskarters come back laden from the sword-trail!"

A shiver went through the bodies around the fire.

"A messenger? To the Gods? Outlander," said the voice of Rajn, "who would carry such a message to the Gods?"

"I have someone," said Harb.

Without hesitating he stepped back and to one side, drew his sword, and struck with it at the neck of the male slave behind him. The technologically sophisticated blade took the slave's head completely off, and the body fell. With a cry, the plains woman fell on her knees beside the body; and without hesitating, Harb struck again, stretching her lifeless above the dead man.

"You saw and heard," said Harb to the Homskarter, "the woman loved the man, therefore her ghost will follow his. He will be your messenger to

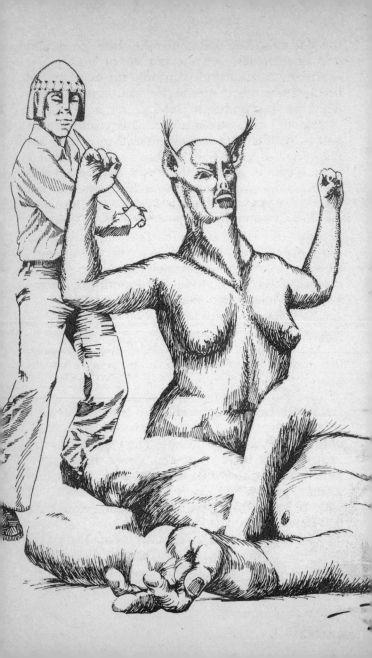

the Gods and she will come after him to witness that what he says is truly your intent."

There was a second with only the crackling of the fire to be heard. All the Homskarters were staring at the two bodies.

"Outlander," said Rajn very slowly into the silence, "I think you should leave us now. You are not one of us and we will talk of our Gods alone."

Harb turned and went off. He went a good distance off, as had become his habit since he had discovered Witta following him. His equipment showed him a way through the pitch-dark woods to a spot in which he did not think any number of Homskarters were likely to find him before dawn. Curling up in a comfortable hollow, he set the thermostat on his clothing to keep him at a comfortable warmth, and fell asleep.

In the morning, he rejoined the natives, and they started out on the last half-day of travel that would bring them home to the Homskarter village. Neither Rajn nor any of the others said anything to him. However, he noticed that a cairn of rocks had been raised and the bodies of the two he had slain were laid on top of it, out of the reach of animals. This was the procedure of the forest people in offering sacrifices to the Gods; and there could be only one reason why those two bodies were being treated as sacrifices. Harb smiled.

They continued on home. There, once the festivities of their return were over, Rajn spoke once more privately to Harb.

"It may be," said the king, "seeing you're of the same kind as the Other who scratches in the dirt with those cast off from our own people, that you, like him, know something of the growing of grain. Therefore, since it was a wish of yours to see us supplied with growing fields, suppose you take over the direction of these slaves and make them produce."

Harb had not bargained for the job of agricultural director, but things were going too much in the way he had planned for him to raise objections. Even though it did not take more than a half an eye to see Rajn's true reason in putting him to work. If the fields and all that derived from them should prosper, then that would be all to the credit of the wise ruler who had permitted such an undertaking. While if anything should go wrong, then it must obviously be a case of the Gods, dealing with the impious outlander who had dared to suggest delaying their expected sacrifice.

Harb did not blame Rajn for this particular ploy. It was, he thought, gazing at the king's retreating back, exactly what he would have done in Rajn's place. Rajn and he were both clever minds; and all-powerful as the king seemed to be, it was necessary that he keep safely always on the side of the majority opinion. Otherwise some ambitious aspirant for the throne might one day be able to head a successful uprising against him. Luckily, in the case of any such happening, Rajn had the four-square respectability of Witta to retreat behind. No one could doubt Witta's devotion to the

traditional ways. But it paid to make doubly safe by having a scapegoat ready, if necessary, as Rajn had just done. Harb respected him for it.

He set about the job, organizing the slaves into two teams, one to clear the land, and one to loosen the earth for planting by jabbing it with the fire-hardened, sharpened ends of sticks. By these primitive methods he managed to clear and prepare fields. Then he put his slaves to the process of drilling holes in the loose earth with their pointed sticks, and hand-planting his seed grains.

There seemed to be a different attitude toward him on the part of the slaves now. He could not put his finger on any specific sign of it; but he could feel it, almost like a solid wall of emotion when he was out in the field alone with them. Helmeted, armored and with sword and shield, he had nothing to fear from even fifty of them. Nonetheless, he began to be aware that if he should show any sign of weakness or fear, the slaves nearby would be on him like predators upon a wounded prey.

It puzzled him for a while. The slaves had shown no such deep hatred for the Homskarters. Then he realized where the roots of their feeling lay. They had all come to know how he had sacrificed two of them at the camp the evening before their arrival here, and that knowledge had triggered off an emotional reaction in them reserved for him alone. To these people of the plains, the forest warriors were a natural disaster. When they came and killed you mourned the dead, but that was all. Raiders were something to be endured, like a flood or a stroke of lightning.

But Harb was not something natural. He was alien, strange. To be killed by him was an unthinkable thing; while to kill him was instinctive reflex, as it might be instinct to kill a poisonous snake, even though it was not threatening you at the moment. Understanding this, for the first time Harb realized why Rajn, alone of the Homskarters, had ever had much to do with him. The Homskarters must have an instinctive antipathy for him, also; an antipathy that was personified in Witta, and which explained that individual's actions toward Harb.

It was curious, thought Harb suddenly, as he stood in the late afternoon sun on one of his fields beside the lake and watched the slaves drilling individual holes with their pointed sticks to take two grains apiece of the cereal they were planting, but the antipathy the Homskarters showed to him seemed to be entirely missing from them in the case of Bill Cohone. True, they made fun of the Volunteer and scorned those of their own kind who went to work with him; but clearly not only those natives Cohone had "converted", but the rest of the Homskarters had no dislike for the amateur human xenosociologist. In fact, just the contrary. They seemed almost to have the sort of amused contempt for Cohone that bordered on a near-affection; for no good reason that Harb could see — except that Cohone had more or less fallen in with the role of buffoon as the natives saw it.

All the same, thought Harb, it was too bad matters were not the other way around, with the natives hating Cohone and not disliking him. He had now done almost everything he had set out to accomplish. In a few months there would be grain to harvest, giving the Homskarters a tradeable surplus. This wealth would make life good for them, for which they would give credit to the Gods and assume that the taking of slaves and the growing of grain was not only profitable but blessed. Wealth, inevitably, would breed power. The Homskarters were on the way to ruling all the forest tribes and eventually forging an army of conquest that would go down to occupy and rule the kingdom of the plains. Pre-history here on 49381D was all but nudged, now, into a new, accelerated path.

However, meanwhile, there remained the matter of tidying up. It was quite true, as he had told Cohone, that the private rule of the emerging professional group among those who operated on the stellar frontiers was "survival of the fittest" and that the rule was not to avoid breaking the rules, but to make sure that if you broke them, you gained more than the rule-breaking cost. Harb's own professional superiors would wink at his bringing in and using the tools of a high technology among these primitives just as long as his doing so got results and accelerated the local growth toward civilization. By getting results, even at the cost of breaking rules Harb would have fulfilled the harsh letter of the fittest-survival code, and his superiors would cooperate in hiding any bad marks that otherwise might appear on his record.

But beyond those superiors, there were the older human worlds, and particularly Earth itself, well-supplied with impractical armchair theoreticians and bleeding-heart types. If some influential individuals of that stamp should get wind through Cohone of what Harb had done with it here; and if a public outcry should be raised, Harb had no doubt his superiors would not hesitate in throwing him to the wolves. By the standard they used he would have failed the survival test.

It followed therefore, that from the beginning Harb had been alive to the necessity of keeping Cohone from talking. That was why it was too bad that Cohone's Homskarters were not just waiting for a chance to kill him, as the slaves were Harb. The rays of the late afternoon sun struck suddenly into Harb's eyes as he turned, charging the landscape around him with the color of blood; and sudden inspiration woke in Harb's mind.

Of course Cohone's converts were not like Harb's slaves — waiting for the first opportunity to kill him — *but no human except Harb himself knew that fact!*

That evening, Harb asked to speak to Rajn privately. They climbed together to the tower that was the scene of their earlier conferences. The summer moon of 49381D was high enough above the horizon to give some light now, and the nighttime air in this season was almost balmy. Above them, the stars twinkled so brightly they seemed almost within reach of an upstretched arm.

"What is it, Outlander?" Rajn asked.

"A small problem, King," said Harb. "He whom you call the Other has become jealous of me because I am growing more grain then he has been able to do with his handful of followers."

Rajn stared at him. In the moonlight the

Homskarter's round face was clearly visible, but his eyes were ovals of jet, unreadable.

"How do you know this, Outlander?" Rajn said. "You haven't been close to your fellow since we left on the sword-trail."

"We of our kind know much of what each other is thinking," Harb said. "It's one of our ways. I tell you, king, about this only because the Other may now do something to cause my fields to fail, or the slaves to die, so that they would not be available for the harvest, and the sacrifice to follow."

"How could he do such things?"

"I don't know yet," said Harb. "But he may have some means that is *magic*."

Harb paused deliberately before the last word to make sure that the king understood. But he need not have worried. There was nothing dull about the perceptions of the Homskarters' ruler.

"I see," said Rajn slowly. "Surely now, that would be something unfortunate. One magic bowl and one magic sword is enough magic for this kingdom. Nor would it be agreeable to me to lose the grain that you will grow; and very unhappy indeed it would be to have the slaves die before they could be properly sacrificed. What does the outlander think can be done about his brother up-lake?"

"I'll go talk to him," said Harb. "Perhaps I can find out what he plans to do. Then I'll come back and talk some more with the king. I've hesitated to do this until now because I've got no one besides myself to look after the slaves while I'm gone."

"Don't concern yourself about that." The jet ovals of Rajn's vision narrowed thoughtfully. "I'd already planned, I remember now, to take them from you for a day or two and put them to work at cleaning and mending the canots."

"That's good, King," said Harb. "I'll leave first thing in the morning, then."

He was at Cohone's station by two hours after sunrise the next day. It looked, except for lack of gray in the forest greenery, that had passed with the change of season, no different than it had looked before. Only, the crops in Cohone's small field, obvious fruit of planting late the previous fall, were now standing tall and almost ready for harvesting so that a second planting could be gotten in.

Harb smiled internally, however, at the number of the Homskarters he saw around the station. Instead of the four that had been there when Harb landed, Harb now saw more than a dozen. It was not the sort of increase that indicated any sudden new success on Cohone's part in recruiting the natives to ways of primitive agriculture and industry, but any increase at all could be argued in evidence to substantiate what Harb had told Rajn the night before.

Bill Cohone was supervising what seemed to be the digging of a well. Like the rest of the scene, he could almost have stepped just now out of the moment of Harb's landing. Shirtless, half-bald, red-faced and undernourished-looking, he broke off what he was doing to come down to the landing as Harb drove the prow of his small canot ashore with the outboard motor still attached to it.

"I've been hearing about you," Cohone said, as Harb stepped ashore and started up toward the building that was both Cohone's home and head-quarters.

"Oh?" said Harb. "I didn't know you had a phone link to other parts of this planet."

"Don't try to make a joke out of it!" said Cohone, following beside Harb as he climbed the slight slope from the water to the building. "My converts hear from the other Homskarters, and tell me. And lately Witta's dropped by to give me some of the details about what happened on that expedition to the plains. You're a murderer!"

"It depends on how you define whoever's killed," said Harb. He reached the door of the building and put his hand on the leather strap that latched it. "I've got a call to put in to Sector headquarters. I don't suppose you'd consider resigning for reasons of health?"

"Like hell!" Cohone's hands were clenched. The skin of them was as usual dirt-stained and their bones were larger than his skinny body would have indicated. The knobby fists he made were not ridiculous. "Is that what you came for?"

"I told you — I came here to put in a private call to Sector," said Harb, opening the door. "Do you mind?"

Cohone stood back, scowling. Harb went in, closing the door behind him. He found himself in a large single room that was hardly more than a primitive cabin, except for the bank of powerful interstellar communications equipment in one far corner. He went to the equipment, sat down, put a headset and throat mike on, and keyed in Sector Headquarters.

There was a short wait. Even with a relay satel-

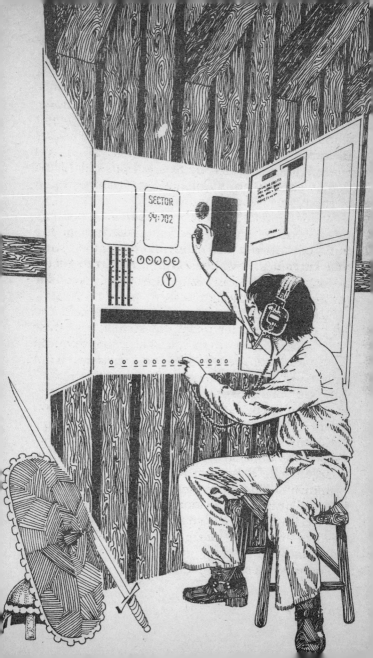

lite in orbit around the planet and the newest of phase-shift equipment, a trans-light call of some twenty parsecs was not made immediately. But then the ready light on the control face of the equipment lit up redly.

"This is Sector," said a voice from the speaker within the bones of Harb's inner ear. "Come in, 49381D. Go ahead, Cohone."

"Sector Chief Mallard speaking," said Harb, dryly. "I'm just using Cohone's equipment to put in a call."

"Oh, sorry sir."

"All right. Listen, Cohone isn't looking too well, I think he's been overworking and over-identifying, rubbing these locals the wrong way. I suggested he resign for health reasons, or at least a leave of absence, but he wouldn't go for it. Would you get a medical officer in here to have a look at him?"

"Right away, Chief."

"Good. No need to get Cohone worked up. Why don't you send the pod in as if it were a routine delivery of something like updated communication equipment, and not mention that the Med's aboard. That way the Med can get a good look before Cohone has a chance to tighten up on him."

"Yes sir."

"Good. I'll be finishing up here in about two more months, myself. Any emergencies in my office?"

"No sir. Deputy Chief's advisory says everything's going routinely."

Harb silently blessed his choice of an ambitious young Deputy Chief who thought he stood a chance to taking over Harb's job one of these days when Harb himself was promoted.

"Good. So much for now. Out."

"Out."

Harb shut off the equipment and went back outside the building. Cohone was nowhere to be seen. Harb hesitated, wondering whether to wait for the man and talk to him a while for appearances sake, so that the word of their interview would be taken back to Rajn. But after all, they had had some conversation in their own tongue while walking up from the canot, and that was probably enough gossip to be relayed back to the Homskarter king.

He took his canot and went back to the village. Once there, he sought out Rajn.

"King," he said, "I'm afraid I wasn't able to find out just what the Other is going to do to your slaves and crops, but it's very clear that he plans to destroy both."

"Stop him, Outlander."

"I can't," said Harb.

Rajn's voice was as cold with suspicion as if Harb were a stranger encountered for the first time.

"Why not? Is he stronger than you?"

"No," said Harb. "He's nothing, compared to me. But he has friends. Not great friends, or many friends, but enough to make it impossible for me to stop him at this time."

Rajn stared at him.

"Are you seeking a price from me, Outlander?"

"No," said Harb. "It's not a matter of price. It's just that in this instance I can't help you. But, King . . . you can help yourself."

"I?"

"If his crops should be flattened, and all those at his place should be slain —"

Rajn coughed dry laughter.

"You should know me better, Outlander," he said. "I'm not a fool, to kill your brother for you when you dare not kill him yourself."

"No — I don't mean that the Other should be slain," Harb said. "Only that those of your own people who have fallen away from you to be with him should die. Then he'd have nothing to do here; and he'd have to leave."

Rajn stood motionless in silence for nearly a full minute. It was impossible for Harb to guess what the Homskarter was thinking.

"He's done us no harm so far," Rajn said. "And I've only your word for it that he intends harm, now."

"Hasn't my word been good also, so far?" demanded Harb. "And besides, isn't a wise ruler one who takes care of trouble before it can begin? Also, King, what have you got to lose — a handful of your own people who aren't actually even your own any longer?"

Once more Rajn thought.

"All right," he said abruptly. "But it won't be easy to find someone to lead warriors against some who were once our own people."

"I thought of that," said Harb. "Surely, there are two whom your warriors would follow into anything. Yourself, and Witta."

Rajn stared at him with dark eyes.

"Neither I, nor Witta, for this," said the Homskarter king. "But I will find someone. And may the

Gods help you, Outlander, if you have counseled me badly in this doing."

The following morning, early, Witta took a hunting party into the woods at the King's request. Shortly thereafter Harb took his small canot and started once more uplake in the direction of Cohone's station, following about an hour behind a good-sized body of warriors in three large canots who had left earlier in that direction, shortly after Witta's group was gone. Harb drove his canot to within half a mile of the station, then beached it under the cover of some overhanging brush and made his way on foot up to the fringe of the forest from which he could look into the cleared area that held the fields and the station.

The fields were silent. What lay among the stems of the tall grain it was impossible to say, but close to the main building on the open ground were what might have been bundles of rags lying on the ground, showing here and there the colors used in non-royal Homskarter body, arm and leg wrappings.

Harb set himself patiently to watch. An hour or so went by and the sun warmed. Finally, the door to the building opened by slow jerks and the head of Cohone peered out, followed slowly by his full figure. He stood before the door and stared about him, at the apparent bundles of rags. Slowly, he moved to examine them, one by one. He walked like a drunken man; and after he had gazed at the last one he could find, he stood and stared downlake toward the Homskarter village for a long time. Then he went back inside.

Harb stayed where he was, waiting. Late that

afternoon, Cohone reappeared, carrying a piece of equipment which the rules required be kept securely out of native hands — a collapsible metal shovel, now extended into working position. With this, he dug holes in the earth and attempted, one by one, to bury the rag bundles. But the effort seemed to drain him of strength, and when it began to get dark, he stopped with two bodies still not interred. He went back inside; and Harb found a comfortable patch of earth under a tree, set his clothing thermostat 'at a sleeping temperature, and dropped off into slumber.

With sunrise, he renewed his watch. About mid-morning a pod descended from an interstellar aircraft and the pilot, together with another man wearing the white shoulder patch of the Medical Arm, left it, came to the building and let themselves in. A second later, Harb heard faintly the sound of hysterical yelling from the building, and Cohone burst out of the door, running toward the grain fields. The two men followed, caught him, and did something to him. Suddenly Cohone went limp. The others carried him to the pod, shut the hatch behind them, and the pod took off, to lose itself in the brilliant blue of the summer sky.

Harb stood up, stretched with satisfaction and walked back to his canot. As he drove the canot with the outboard motor back towards the Homskarter village, his feeling of satisfaction grew. Cohone's testimony would be suspect from now on; particularly in view of the fact that Harb had asked for medical help for him two days before his mismanagement of his station resulted in the massacre of his converts by the wild natives. It was a bonus that Cohone had evidently grown close enough to his converts so that seeing them slaughtered had driven him into a real state of emotional shock. Of course, they could cure him in a few days but that would not change anything. The view he had acquired here on the planet would remain suspect. In a couple of days Harb could drop by the station, be shocked himself by what he found and call Sector Headquarters, to be more shocked by what he was told of Cohone's emotional condition. It was all tied up, now. Mission accomplished.

Harb reached the village and tethered his canot at the wharf. There were only a couple of older male villagers armed and on duty there, and these did not answer when he spoke to them. Harb guessed that they would by now have heard of the raid on the station, and perhaps these two had owned a friend or relative among the converts. Harb ignored them and went up through the near-empty streets to the house of the king.

The doors of the big house were open and two other Homskarters Harb did not recognize were on duty. From within came the sounds of a very large celebration taking place, rather than the ordinary afternoon drinking and arguing. Harb went up the steps without bothering to speak to the new guards and stepped inside. The main hall was packed with warriors, shouting, laughing, and drinking.

Harb started down the open center lane between tables that led to the small table of the king, blinking his eyes in the dimness to get the dazzle of the sunlight out of them. It was a technique he had become expert in since returning from the expedition to the plains.

Abruptly, all sound in the hall died away. Harb was surrounded by total and unexpected silence. He stopped, blinking furiously, and slowly the scene became clear around him.

On every side, warriors were leaning forward, staring at him, motionless. A dozen steps in front of him, for he had covered almost half the distance through the hall automatically, stood the table of the king. But Rajn was not behind it. There was only Witta, who sat staring at Harb as the warriors stared.

There was something strange about those stares; something possibly — not for the first time Harb cursed the fact that the Homskarter features were all but impossible for a human to read emotion from — savage and triumphant. Obviously some unusual event had taken place, but what? Whatever it was seemed to be connected with the fact that Rajn was absent. Could Witta have taken advantage of some short trip of the king's to set the Homskarters here to taking some sort of action against Harb? It was unthinkable that Witta should suppose he should get away with such a thing. Once the king returned, Rajn would have to take action himself against Witta, if only to reestablish the fact that his authority was not to be flouted.

On the other hand, these primitives were sometimes incredibly stupid about the future results of their present actions. Harb came to a decision. If Witta was trying anything, the thing to do was to

face the vice-king down sharply and decisively, right now before the situation had a chance to gather momentum.

Keeping his eyes on Witta's, Harb stepped out and strode briskly forward toward the table. He was almost to it, when he stumbled and almost went down, checking himself just before he fell over something that he had not noticed until now, lost as it was in the shadows of the reed-strewn floor.

He looked down. The body of a Homskarter lay at his feet. Blood from more than a dozen wounds had dyed red the white wrappings of arms, and legs, and the upper body. The head lolled to one side, grimacing in death. It was Rajn.

Harb stared down, unbelieving. What he was looking at could not be. He raised his head to demand that Witta tell him what had happened; but the first sounds from his throat were drowned in the gleeful roar with which the warriors came pouring over their tables to hurl him down and pin him to the floor.

CHAPTER TEN

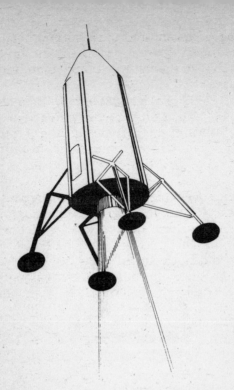

Nearly a week later what seemed at first to be a small sun came down from the sky to hover over the Homskarter town. A mighty voice that was the voice of Cohone spoke to the Homskarters in their own tongue, saying that he and some other outlanders would descend and move among them and by no means was any Homskarter to interfere with any of those who would land.

At this, all those in the village began to shake with fear. They crouched low on the ground and tried not to look when a small flying box such as had been used to come down to Cohone, descended, and three outlanders got out. One was Cohone himself; and seeing him, some of the braver warriors ventured to raise their heads and watch as the three went past them and up to the king's house, to the tall tree from which hung the woven cage.

"Allah!" said one of the other two, a female outlander with jet-black hair and a white patch on the shoulder of her upper garment, gazing at the thing inside the cage. "Let's get him down from there."

The third outlander, a male like Cohone, undid the knot that held the rope by which the cage was raised into position with a new occupant. The cage came to the ground, the rope holding the door to it shut was cut through, and the three reached in. The creature that had been Harb, however, did not want to come out. It cried and crouched away from them; but by main strength they got it from the cage and the one with the patch on her shoulder touched it with a small glass tube, after which it became quiet and very docile; and she was able to lead it, shambling and crouching, and sometimes even falling, down to the pod.

Cohone and the other male outlander started to follow; but a Homskarter warrior wearing the white wrappings of a king crawled out of the open door of the king's house and came writhing toward them, face down to the dust, up to their very feet. They stopped. The king lifted his face. It was Witta.

"Don't let the devils kill us!" he said to Cohone, clutching at Cohone's ankle. "There was no more we could stand, so we put him in a cage. We did not kill him. We only put him in a cage."

Cohone reached down and urged Witta to his feet.

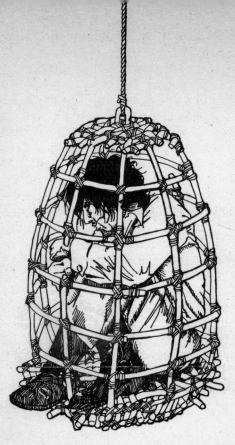

"The devils won't kill you," he said, gently. But Witta still clutched him, now by the arm.

"We've sacrificed all the slaves," Witta said, pleadingly. "I sent people to put back all that was damaged where you lived. There are those who will come to take the place of those killed by the order of Rajn, when he was made mad by the devil we put in the cage. All the fields that the slaves cleared for us have been plucked clean of any growing thing. Only your fields remain with grain still on them. Come back to us. Teach us what to do and we'll do it! But protect us from devils and all terrible things!"

Cohone gently pried Witta's fingers from his arm.

"I'm coming back," he said. "Go tell your people that."

"Thank you. Thank you. Thank . . ." said Witta, backing away. He turned, scrambled to his feet and ran into the dark safety of the king's house.

"You see?" said Cohone, grimly, turning to the man beside him. On that individual, the twin stars of a Departmental General glittered in the yellow sunlight. "Do you believe me now about the effects of what Mallard tried to do?"

"I believe you," the DG nodded. "It's plain enough what he tried. And if he'd succeeded we'd be patting him on the back right now. But it backfired on him — and I still don't understand exactly why. These people haven't developed consciences yet, surely."

"Of course not!" said Cohone. "They've got what came before conscience and was meant to do the same work. *Custom.* I warned Mallard that if he pressed these people too hard, they'd bounce back at him. You realize that was all he did that was unworkable — press them too hard? Everything else was quite acceptable by their standards, the advantage-taking, the enslaving of captives, the killing of helpless people for sacrifice? He only made that one mistake — being too successful."

"Too successful?" the DG raised his sandy eyebrows. He was as tall as Cohone, but more athletically built, in spite of his age — which was perhaps twenty years older than that of the amateur x-sociologist.

"That's what I said." Abruptly, Cohone started to walk back toward the pod and the DG came along with him. "He was giving Rajn advice; and everything he got Rajn to do, worked. Actually, it was Rajn who became too successful. He was doing nothing but breaking custom and coming up covered with roses every time he did it. Finally, he went too far in killing my converts."

"But I thought these village people had no use for the converts?"

"They didn't. But the converts were Homskarters, after all. If killing them turned out to be a successful thing, then who was next to be sacrificed to a change of custom? Custom to these people is like common law was before written statutes — the only machinery there is to make sure the world works right. When it began to look like Rajn could kill his own people and get away with it, that had to be a sign that a devil was loose in the world."

"And we know who the devil was, unfortunately," said the DG.

"Unfortunately," said Cohone, grimly, "so did the Homskarters. So they took the obvious step— replaced Rajn with a conservative king and locked the devil up in a cage where he couldn't cause any more trouble."

"Well, well," said the DG. They were at the entrance to the pod. He stopped. "In any case, it's worked out well. It looks like you'll have them eating out of your hand when you get back here."

Cohone also stopped. He frowned.

"If I do come back," he answered slowly.

The DG looked closely at him.

"If I understand Homskärter," he said, "what you just said to that new king was — "

"But then *you* said," Cohone darted a glance at him, "that if Mallard had been successful you'd be patting him on the back right now. He told me you HQ people were operating privately on a principle of survival of the fittest — that anything anyone could make work would be accepted. I didn't believe it — then. I don't think that way myself; and I don't know that I want to work with people who do."

"Look here, Bill," said the DG, putting his hand on the edge of the open hatch and leaning toward Cohone. He lowered his voice earnestly and confidentially, "Mallard told you the truth, and you might as well face it as a fact. We're a young race, a small race, just beginning to stick our nose out into the universe. How the hell do we know what's right to do when we run across a planet of intelligent non-human locals? A decision's been made arbitrarily that the best thing to do is to help them along toward the same sort of technological civilization that made us what we are today — "

"You needn't go over the rule book with me," broke in Cohone impatiently. "I'm not talking about general principles — "

"But I am," persisted the DG, "because general principles are what's at issue here. I say, the decision's been made to help them along because maybe if we cast our bread on waters it'll come back to us some day when they've reached a civilized level and we need friends. But how do we help them? What's wrong and what's right? We can try to apply our own ethical and moral stan-

dards, but who knows if that's the best thing for
them?"

"It's better than survival of the fittest," said
Cohone, "which is just another way of saying what
works is justified — after the act."

"Exactly," said the DG.

"Well, it didn't work here," said Cohone with
near-savage satisfaction. He pointed into the pod.
"Go take another look at your success story."

"He's not a success story," said the DG.

"You just said he was."

"No," said the DG. "You said he was. From our
standpoint he ended by failing. That wipes him
out. Survival of the fittest means just what it says.
His way failed. Your way, judging from what that
local said back there, is working."

He poked a rigid finger into Cohone's chest.

"You're the success," he said. "So we go with
you — until something trips you up and *you* fail.
And you'll go along with us — or else regret to
your dying day that you didn't finish up what

you've started here with these people."

He withdrew his finger and stepped away through the hatch into the pod, leaving Cohone alone in the sunlight.

"Coming?" he asked from within the shadow of the hatch. "Or staying?"

"I'll call for transport when I need it," answered Cohone harshly. "Right now I've got to clean up the mess your professional left."

Manai Elles, the white Med Service patch on her jacket shoulder taking the sunlight brilliantly as she stepped back out of the pod, emerged and turned to speak to the DG.

"Mallard's quiet. He'll be easy to handle up at the station," she said. "I'd better make some physiological tests of these natives while I'm here, just in case there was some off-world contamination as a result of Mallard's fun and games. I'll call for transport myself as soon as I need it — possibly a day or two."

"Very well," said the DG from within. A moment later the hatch closed and the pod lifted, dwindling rapidly to nothingness in the blue of the sky. Cohone looked at Manai penetratingly for a second, but her face was calm. He turned away to look back at the village, where a few timid faces were beginning to peer more bravely from doorways and windows.

"I've got to get the station here back on a working basis," he said — aloud, but not looking at Manai. "Right now Witta and the others are ready to fall all over themselves to please me. But I've got to nail down the lessons they learned from having Harb among them, while the effect's still strong."

"So," said Manai. "You'll be staying after all."

Cohone laughed, a little bitterly.

"Staying?" he looked at her, at that. "Of course I'm staying. Mallard was just what I needed here — just the sort of leverage I'd been praying for and couldn't get through official channels."

She gazed steadily at him and put her hand on his arm almost soothingly.

"What do you mean?" she asked gently.

"Mean?" Cohone's laugh was still bitter. "I mean I'm a monster — a thoroughly bloody-minded person, ten times as bad as Mallard was!"

He stared at her for a moment, then began to talk quickly, almost angrily.

"Don't you think I saw through him from the first? From the first I knew what was going to happen if he tried what he wanted to try. He was an innocent — an innocent with a diploma! I wanted him to try it, so I could use the results — don't you see?"

"You warned him — "

"Of course I warned him. I warned him, knowing he wouldn't listen. And I knew that someone trying what he'd decided to try would have made sure Sector Headquarters and any other superior post wouldn't know what was going on here, or wouldn't become alerted in time to interfere. He didn't want any interference. He!"

"Were you that sure it would all work out just like this?"

"I knew it would work out to this kind of a result." Suddenly he looked at her almost appealingly. "I couldn't let the chance pass, the chance to replace an intelligent, but dangerous king like Rajn — who was hard to handle — with a dull-witted conservative like Witta, who could be maneuvered within the official guidelines — safely within the cultural pattern. And I was able to get away with using him because it was he who was the amateur — he who didn't know what dynamite he was playing with when he tried to change a people like this, all at once, by main force!"

"It's all right," said Manai. "He was wrong and tried to do the wrong thing. You tried to do the right thing and it came out right."

"But I made myself worse than he was, in order to do it. I went along with it, knowing what it would cost him, what it would cost in the lives of Homskarters and others — " he broke off, and laughed again. But for the first time his laugh was more weary then bitter.

"Ah, hell!" he said. "It's done! Now things can go forward. I'm a bloody-minded man, all right, but it's a bloody-minded culture here, and I've lived with it all these years."

"You're not a bloody-minded man," said Manai. "Don't tell yourself that unless you really want to be one."

"Well, I don't." He sighed, but again he sounded more weary than bitter. "All right, perhaps I'm not yet thoroughly there yet. But I've reached the point where I wanted results, I simply went after them and got them, never mind the cost."

Manai did not seem convinced. She looked at him closely.

"You loved Rajn, didn't you?" she said. "He was your friend. In fact, you love all these people."

He started. Almost, he shied away from her.

"Me? Love them? God, no!" he said, explosively. "I can barely stand the sight of them, after all these years!"

He turned abruptly from her, and went striding off, back into the village.

"Witta!" he shouted, his voice hard. "Witta, come out here! There's things you're going to have to do from now on, if I'm going to make you people safe from devils like the last one — and a lot of the other troubles you're always getting yourselves into, too!"